207102

find my way home

mark timlin

find my way home

VICTOR GOLLANCZ

LONDON

First published in Great Britain 1996
by Victor Gollancz
An imprint of the Cassell Group
Wellington House, 125 Strand, London WC2R 0BB

A catalogue record for this book is
available from the British Library.

ISBN 0 575 06300 9

Typeset by CentraCet Ltd, Cambridge
Printed and bound in Great Britain by
St Edmundsbury Press Ltd, Bury St Edmunds, Suffolk

96 97 98 99   10 9 8 7 6 5 4 3 2 1

This book is for Billy Chainsaw,
Cathi Unsworth and Ian Johnston,
who've given me more laughs than
a barrowload of monkeys.
And Shend, who taught me
how to ride a motorbike over
the phone.

Everyone is damaged

1

They found Harry Stonehouse's head in a black plastic bag on a barge carrying garbage to some Godforsaken part of Essex to use as landfill. Personally I can't think of anything better to do with the whole county than to fill it with shit. Who'd notice a little more? His teeth had been smashed out to confuse identification. They found his torso in Stamford Bridge. They found his right hand in a skip in Waterloo, the tips of his fingers neatly sheared off to cause more confusion, and his left leg under a bush in Regent's Park. They never did find his left hand or right leg. Probably eaten by animals was the conclusion.

Harry always was a geezer who liked to get around. And even brown bread he managed it.

It took a while to find all the bits they did find, and a week or two more to identify him.

I read about it in the *Standard*, eating an ice-cream in Brockwell Park on a warm summer evening in the middle of a free Reggae concert.

It was the previous night's paper, and I picked it up off the grass and gave it a quick scan as I walked through the crowd getting a contact high from all the spliff being smoked.

I was looking for a bloke who'd done a runner with his brother's credit cards, and I'd been told he was a big fan of Aswad, who were topping the bill.

When I saw the story about Harry on page three of the

9

paper I thought, my, my, doesn't the past have a habit of jumping up and socking you in the mouth when you least expect it?

I threw the paper into a bin with the remains of the ice-cream, and kept on going. I never did find the geezer's brother, or the cards, or get paid for my time, but I didn't care. I didn't care about a lot of things in those days. Everything and everyone I had cared for was dead or gone. Except for my daughter Judith, of course, and sometimes I woke up from nightmares that she had gone too. The sheets would be wet with sweat, and I'd have to stop myself from phoning to make sure she was OK.

I forgot about Harry after that, until, a couple of months later, along came a phone call that put him right back on my front page.

2

It was about half eleven on a Friday morning, and I was deep into my weekday routine, which was to go down to my office, tear up the junk mail and sit and look at a phone which hardly ever rang, until about noon when I went to the pub without switching on the ansaphone.

That was weekdays. Weekends I spent in my flat in the company of Messrs wine, beer, vodka, gin and Jack Daniel's, with the assistance of Messrs tonic and Coca-Cola, dining on takeouts, and letting the tin containers pile up in the sink until they went green, just in case my old cat ever came back to lick them clean. Up there the phone wasn't even switched on most of the time.

I picked up the receiver, half expecting a double-glazing salesman, when a female voice said: 'Nick?'

'Yeah.'

'It's Nancy. Nancy Stonehouse.'

Jesus, I thought. Chickens coming home to roost.

'Hello, Nancy,' I said. 'Long time.'

Nancy Stonehouse. Wife, or should I say widow, of the previously mentioned Harry.

Harry had been a copper. I'd known him when I was in the job, a long time ago. We were both younger then, but he'd been older than me. Twelve years, maybe. He was a DI, I was a DC. Worlds apart. Also he'd been straight, and I'd been bent, or as I liked to put it – bentish. Bentish enough to get the old heave-ho, but not bent enough, or perhaps just

11

lucky enough, not to go inside. Which also put us worlds apart, but obviously not that far that we couldn't be mates.

We'd often go for a drink when our shifts allowed, and we became pally enough for him to invite me to a party at his place in Southfields one Saturday night, maybe eight, nine years ago now, before the shit hit the fan, and I was given my P45 and no references.

That was where I met Nancy. She was older than me, but younger than him. Good-looking, blonde, slim, but built with amazing legs. And she knew all about them. Enough to show them off in short dresses and high heels, anyway. And she liked to drink and flirt, and so did I.

So, almost inevitably it seemed, we had an affair. For a few months I fucked her every way I knew how, and she did the same, and taught me some new ones, getting all hot and steamy in little hotels all over south London, and one memorable weekend when Harry was on a course, at the Grand Hotel in Brighton.

But as all good things must, it came to an end. No pyrotechnics, no recriminations, just a slow death. And one day I realized that neither of us had phoned the other for weeks, and I filed it away in my back pages with so many other things.

'I heard about Harry,' I said. 'I'm sorry.'

'Thanks. I heard about your wife too. That was terrible.'

'Yeah.'

I don't like to talk about that, so I let the word hang.

'You're a private detective now,' she said.

'When I can be bothered.'

'You're lucky to have the option.'

'I have some money.'

That was about all I did have. Some money and a load of memories.

'Good for you. When did you last hear from Harry?' Change of subject. Right down to business. That was Nancy.

I thought about it. 'I dunno,' I said. 'It's been quite a while.'

Harry had put in twenty years on the force, taken an early retirement, and walked straight into a good job at a security firm. 4F it was called. Which I always thought meant that you couldn't be called up for the army, but in their case apparently stood for: Fraternity, Fortitude, Faith and Fearlessness, though I'd heard other euphemisms which I'll leave to your imagination.

Harry had kept in touch with me through all my ups and downs, constantly suggesting that we met up for a drink, and I for my part was constantly putting him off. I *had* been screwing his wife after all, and even I have my standards. One of which is not to go out drinking with a bloke I've been making a bloody fool of.

'I need to see you. I've been calling,' said Nancy. 'You never seem to be there.'

I ignored the implied rebuke and said, 'You *have* been keeping up with my life.'

'Hardly. There are such things as phonebooks, Nick. Even for that lonely outpost you call home.'

I ignored that comment too. 'What do you want to see me about?' I asked.

'Not on the phone. I'll come to you. Say an hour.'

'You've got the address?' I was rather hoping she hadn't, and I could lie.

'It was in the book too.'

And she hung up.

3

She rolled up exactly fifty-seven minutes later in a red, chauffeur-driven Volvo. The driver was the full half-hour, peaked cap, dark suit and all, and as soon as the car stopped, he jumped out and opened the rear door.

I watched her through the window of my office as she emerged from the motor. Still good-looking, and all neat in black stockings, black high-heeled pumps, black two-piece and little black hat, with her blonde hair pulled up severely under it. The complete mourning kit.

She looked through the window at me, nodded, crossed the road, and I jumped up and opened the door.

Ever the gentleman.

'Nancy,' I said.

'Nick,' she replied, and popped up on tippy-toes to kiss my cheek.

'Sit down,' I invited her. 'A drink of something?'

'Got any scotch?'

'No. But the pub's open. I'll nip over.' Nip over for a nip, I thought.

'We could talk there, couldn't we?'

'Why not?' I said, and we went out together, crossed the road past the Volvo where the driver gave me a sneer through the windscreen, and I gave him a sneer back, and into the boozer, which was almost empty at that hour. Dionne Warwick was singing 'Do You Know The Way To

San José?' on the stereo. We found a seat in the corner and I went to the bar.

I paid for two large scotches, mimed the water jug and Nancy nodded. I added a drop of liquid to each glass and took them over to where she was sitting and plonked them down on the table.

'Long time,' I said when I was seated and smoking, after offering the pack to Nancy, her shaking her head, me asking if she minded if I smoked, and lighting up after she shook her head again.

Such modern times.

'You said that before,' she riposted.

'It's a habit of mine,' I said. 'Repeating myself.'

'I remember.'

Was that an insult or a compliment? I took it as the latter.

'Yours?' I asked.

'What?'

'The Volvo.'

'No. Miles and Miles Hire. I don't like mini-cabs. It's cheap too.'

And comes complete with a young, virile driver, I thought, but said nothing.

We sipped our drinks and she looked round the bar.

'So what can I do for you?' I asked.

'You said you hadn't heard from Harry for a long time. How long?'

'Eighteen months, maybe two years,' I replied.

'You're sure?'

'Sure I'm sure.'

'I hadn't heard from him for a year.'

I thought about it. 'Really?' I said.

'Really.'

'Was this intentional?'

She shook her head, and one strand of blonde hair broke loose from the bun at the back of her head and drifted down to the collar of her suit where it caressed the line of her neck. It looked most attractive, as it happened, and I remembered what Nancy and I had done together all those years ago.

'No,' she said. 'One day he just went off to work as usual, or at least I thought it was as usual. An hour later I found his Jag was still parked in the garage. I phoned the office and he hadn't arrived. I found his car and house keys on the kitchen cabinet. Now, he'd never go anywhere without that car normally. He loved the sodding thing.'

'And?'

'And nothing. That was it. He vanished. Left everything behind. Passport, birth certificate, chequebook, credit cards, the lot.'

'Cash?'

'He never touched our bank account after that day. Maybe he had fifty, sixty quid on him.'

'And he never got in touch?'

'Never.'

'How did you feel about that?'

She shrugged. 'I couldn't've cared less, really. Our marriage had been over for years. We were just too lazy to do anything about it. Harry went his way, I went mine. You know all about that.'

I did. But she still wore black for him. I wondered why.

'Were you all right for money?'

'Sure. Better than I thought we were really.'

And that was when I should have asked the obvious question, but didn't. Out of practice, see.

'So he hadn't been milking the family finances in order to do a runner?'

She shook her head.

'Did you go to the police?'

'Of course.'

'And?'

'Nothing. They put him on the national register of missing people . . . persons. And then nothing.'

'What else did you do?'

'Went to the Sally Army. Not that I could see Harry sleeping rough, or dossing in one of their hostels. Then I left it.'

'Broken-hearted, like.'

'Don't take the piss, Nick. I figured he'd sorted out some other life and gone to live it.'

'And now?

'Now I don't know. Whoever killed him certainly meant it.'

That was for sure, and I shivered slightly at the thought.

'So why me?' I asked.

As if I didn't know.

'I want you to find out what happened to that year.'

My heart sank.

'But the Old Bill must be on the case now.'

'They don't seem to care . . .'

And then she started crying.

Shit, I thought. The old waterworks. I should've known.

'But he's ex-job,' I said. 'A good copper. Popular.'

She shrugged, and I thought about it. Very odd if she was right. Now if *I* turned up in bits and pieces all over the greater metropolitan area, it'd be free drinks all round at the police social club.

But Harry.

Strange. Very strange.

'So will you help?' she asked. 'I can pay. There's life policies. I'm not broke.'

'I'll have to think about it,' I said.

'I can make it worth your while,' she said, and crossed her legs. I heard the rasp of nylon on nylon over Dionne doing 'A House Is Not A Home'.

I knew just what she meant, and Nancy too.

4

Not that I was exactly short of female company. About seven months after my wife died I met a woman. Her name is Diane Murphy and she's a secretary in an investment firm on the edge of the City, and far too young for me. It had only been a brief meeting, the first one, and it took me three months to get round to calling her, but I hadn't asked a woman out for a long time and I was a bit rusty.

I got through to a female switchboard operator at the company.

'Can I speak to Diane, please?' I asked.

'Diane who?'

I didn't know. I told you it had been a brief meeting, and I didn't even know if she still worked there.

'I don't know,' I said. 'She's a secretary. Tall, with long, dark hair. Sorry, this is stupid. I met her downstairs in the pub some time ago. She gave me this number.' She hadn't. She'd told me the name of the firm as I was leaving the boozer. It had been a stressful moment, but I'd remembered it, and looked up the number in the book.

There was a brief pause at the other end, and I knew I'd either got an ally, or someone who thought I was a nutter.

'Hold on,' said the voice, and I heard a click, and I was in on hold limbo with some orchestral version of a Billy Joel tune tinkling in my ear.

I was just about to abandon the call, when the tune ended abruptly, and another female voice said: 'Yes.'

19

'Diane?'

'Yes.' The voice sounded uninterested.

'Erm . . .' I told you I was rusty. 'We met some time ago. You asked me to call you.'

'Did I?'

'Yes. My name's Nick. Nick Sharman.'

'Really. I meet a lot of people.'

I was sure she did, and her voice was still uninterested.

'I'm a detective. There was a bit of trouble.'

She finally let me off the hook, but not before my palms were sweating, and my armpits were hot. 'I remember,' she said. 'You're the one with the boots.'

'That's right.'

'You took your time.'

'Sorry . . . ?'

'Phoning.'

'Yeah. It's a long story.'

'They usually are.'

'I wondered if you fancied a drink some night?'

'I fancy a drink lots of nights.'

'With me, I meant.'

'I didn't think you meant with my mum.'

'Do you?'

'What?'

She was making me pay for the delay.

'Fancy a drink?'

'Are you going to beat up any of my friends this time?'

'I didn't mean to do it last time.'

'It's OK. He was asking for it.'

'Does he bear a grudge?'

'I don't know. But it doesn't matter. He's gone to pastures new.'

'So *do* you?' I wondered if we'd have to go round the houses again, but we didn't.

'OK,' she said. 'When?'

'Whenever you're free.'

'I'm free tonight.'

'So am I.'

'Same place, six o'clock.' I assumed she meant the pub where we'd first met.

'I'll be there,' I said.

And I was. So was she, and she looked every bit as good as I remembered, and I told her the long story over a drink or two, followed by dinner, then I saw her into a cab to Liverpool Street Station. We met again three nights later, and that time she didn't make it to the station. We've been seeing each other off and on since then. Nothing serious. I couldn't handle that, and she knows why, and makes allowances. I'm grateful for that. Grateful for almost anything these days, since my wife was murdered. It takes some getting over, does that. I suppose it's the same when a woman's husband is murdered too, and I saw the pain in Nancy's eyes when she said, 'So will you help me?'

'I don't know. Whoever cut him up into pieces meant business.' Slight understatement there.

'You scared?'

''Course I am.'

'But I need your help. And you owe me something, surely, after all we've been through.'

'That was a long time ago.'

She shrugged helplessly. 'Then you owe Harry. Or at least his memory.'

'Do I?'

She was close to tears by then and she said, 'Or maybe because you owe yourself.'

I thought about that for a bit. 'Maybe I do,' I said.

And looking at Nancy again I suddenly felt very sorry for her and said, 'OK, Nancy. I'll see what I can do, but no promises.'

Never feel sorry for people, especially old lovers. It'll come back and do you up.

It did with me anyway.

5

'Tell me about the day he vanished,' I said.

'I've already told you. He left as usual for his office. At least I thought he did, until I found his car still in the garage when I got mine out to go shopping.'

'When was this exactly?'

'It was a Friday, almost thirteen months ago. A year before his body was found. Or at least most of it.'

Delicate ground, but I had to ask if I was going to do anything for her. 'No hint that anything was up?'

'Not that I noticed. Not that I necessarily would. We were pretty much living apart under one roof by then.'

'And?'

'And what?'

'What did you do then?'

'I called his office. I thought maybe the car wouldn't start, and he'd got a cab off the street. 4F's offices are just over the river in Putney.'

'Why? If you weren't getting on. Why did you bother?'

'You've got to understand the circumstances, Nick. We weren't at each other's throats. He had his life, I had mine. Separate rooms, the whole bit. But we didn't hate each other. We'd been through all that. Sometimes we even had a fuck for old times' sake. It's not unheard of, is it? It suited us both to stay living together, for a lot of reasons. I wanted to know if his mechanic was going to turn up to collect the Jag, and if Harry needed a lift home after work.'

'What did they say?'

'I spoke to his secretary. She said he didn't have any appointments until the afternoon, and she thought maybe he'd just taken the morning off.'

'He could do things like that?'

'He was a director by then. Director in charge of security. He could do more or less what he liked within reason.'

Director in charge of security at a security firm. Nice work if you could get it. 'Good job,' I said.

She nodded.

'So what then?'

'I asked her to get him to call as soon as he arrived. Then I found the car keys.'

'Then?'

'I was a bit surprised. I told you he loved that car. But I assumed there was a good reason. Then after lunch his secretary called me. He'd missed his appointment and that was when I started to get a bit worried.'

'What did you do?'

'I found his address book and I called around a few of his friends. Golfing chums, that sort of thing. Nothing. By that evening I was starting to get . . . Well, annoyed more than anything if you really want to know, and after I'd spoken to Harry's secretary again and found out there'd been no sign of him, I talked to the managing director of 4F. He'd obviously heard that Harry hadn't been into the office all day, and was as mystified as me. He came round that evening on the way home from work. That was when we went through his desk in the study and found his stuff and we decided to call the police.'

'And?'

'A couple of uniforms showed up about two hours later. When they realized who Harry was they called the station and a pair of CID came along. One of them knew Harry from the old days. They asked a lot of questions. I think at first they thought he might've run off with a bimbo, but the fact of who he was, and the fact that the MD of one of the top security firms in the country was there and was dropping the names of the Metropolitan Police Commissioner and the Home Secretary kept them from saying it. I showed them what he'd left behind and they came up with the scenario that he'd been kidnapped and we'd get some kind of call from the kidnappers. You know the sort of thing. Give us the key to the vaults or he dies.'

'But that didn't happen.'

'No. The police kept in close touch all weekend, then on Monday when nothing had happened they seemed to lose interest, and like I said, put him on the register of missing persons.'

'And the firm?'

'Much the same. They paid his salary for three months, then sent a polite letter telling me they wouldn't pay it any more, plus a cheque for his pension contributions, and collected the car.'

'And that was that?'

'Until they found his body.'

'But now the Old Bill must be bopping.'

'Not so's you'd notice.'

Curiouser and curiouser, said Alice, I thought.

'But he's been murdered. Christ, he was in the bloody job.' I scratched my head and lit another cigarette. 'What was the cause of death, by the way?'

'Apart from being chopped into dog food, you mean?'

'Yes, Nancy. Apart from that.'

'He was tortured, then beaten to death.'

'Shit. Sorry. I didn't read that in the papers.'

25

'It hasn't been in the papers.'

'Why not?'

'There hasn't been a formal verdict on the inquest yet. It was adjourned. The same copper who knew Harry before told me that off the record.'

'This is all very odd.'

'You can say that again. Do you think you can do anything, Nick? It's not so much the murder I want you to solve as to find out what he'd been up to since he left.'

'Seems to me they're pretty much one and the same.'

'Not necessarily. Anything could've happened. But you're a man, and used to be in the job yourself. You'll probably have better luck at getting information out of people than I have.'

'I can try,' I said. 'But I tell you now, Nancy, I'm not getting too involved with people who'll torture some poor sod, beat him to death, then cut him up and distribute the pieces all over the shop. I'm trying to give up dangerous sports.'

'You must be getting old, Nick,' she said, and crossed her legs again.

Not as old as all that I thought as I watched her hemline move up her thighs.

'But you will try?'

'I'll have a sniff round. Just for you and Harry.'

'I've got something in here to sweeten the pot,' she said. She opened her handbag and got out a thick brown envelope, and handed it to me. I opened it. It was packed with twenty-pound notes.

'A grand,' she said. 'Should keep you in whatever your poison is these days for a while.'

'Should do,' I said. 'You obviously aren't short.'

She shook her head.

'OK,' I said. 'You've convinced me. Give me the name of your pet cop and the managing director of 4F, and I'll do a little nosing around next week.'

In fact, I was quite looking forward to it. It had been too long.

She gave me the information I'd asked for, and I promised to report in as soon as I found out anything.

She told me I should come round for dinner one night.

I agreed. I wanted to have a shufti round the gaff anyway, and the sound of her nylon-covered legs on top of each other had been getting to me.

Mug punter.

6

As a matter of fact I was seeing Diane that very night, so I mooched the rest of the day away at my office, thinking about what I'd bitten off by agreeing to try and find out what had happened to Harry Stonehouse's lost year.

I'd meant what I'd said about not partaking of dangerous sports any more, and the more I thought, the more I realized I might be getting into hazardous waters. Might? More like undoubtedly would, and by the time I left to meet Diane, I had more or less convinced myself to knock the whole thing on the head, let Nancy know what I'd decided, and give her back the money she'd paid me.

I caught a bus to Blackfriars and walked up into Clerkenwell, where I was due to meet Diane. I told her what had happened but didn't mention my past relationship with Nancy, or indeed that she'd managed to blow some oxygen on to the embers I'd thought were long dead. I didn't feel much commitment to Diane and I doubted that she did to me. She'd had her choice and decided to stick around. That was good, but I didn't want any proper relationship, and if *she* did, that was just too bad. Not a nice attitude, but that was all I could muster. Even so I thought it better to keep shtuum.

We ate in a Korean restaurant in Holborn. Why it stayed open in the evening I'll never know, because the area had emptied out by then, and the few times we'd eaten there before we'd rarely seen any other customers.

It was like that that evening. Being the only two punters in the place, we got our favourite table by the window where we could look out on the traffic heading back and forth across the viaduct.

'It's good to see you interested in something at last,' said Diane, helping herself to some fried noodles in soup, with beef.

'Yeah,' I replied, chewing on a prawn in chilli sauce. 'But I don't know.'

'What?'

'Whether or not to go through with it.'

'Why not?'

I almost choked on the prawn's tail. '*Why not?*' I said. 'Because, like I told you, they're still looking for some bits of Harry, and I don't want to be the next one turning up in black plastic sacks in the back of a garbage truck.'

'But she told you she doesn't want you to find out who killed him. Just what he'd been up to since he left.'

'And of course there's no connection. Come on, Diane, give me a break.'

'Well, it's up to you. But I hate seeing you wasting your life away like you've been doing.'

'I work,' I said defensively.

'About once in a blue moon. What work have you done lately?'

'I was looking for that bloke's car.' A classic Jaguar that had been pinched from outside his house in Dulwich. The police had had no luck, and he called me in. But from the few whispers I'd picked up, it had long gone to Dubai or one of the Emirates by the time I came in on the case.

'And I've done some process serving.'

Diane sniffed.

29

'And there was the bloke who thought his brother had nicked his credit cards.' Just where we came in.

'Wonderful,' said Diane. 'And all that in – how long? Four months, is it?'

'Things are quiet.'

'Sure.'

'OK, Diane, I give in. I don't really want the job. Right now. Any job. At least any job that's going to show a degree of risk.'

'You take a risk every morning when you get up.'

'Which is why I like to sleep in till after lunch.'

'Terrific, Nick. That's a really great attitude.'

I started to get the hump then.

'Who are you to tell me about my attitude?' I said nastily.

'Just a friend.'

'Well. As one friend to another, mind your own damn business.'

I could see I'd hurt her then. She swallowed hard and started to get her stuff together.

I felt like a bastard. 'Diane,' I said, grabbing her hand. 'Don't go. I'm sorry. That was a shitty thing to say. I appreciate what you said. I really do.'

'And?'

I shook my head. She knew she had me cold. 'And I'll see what I can do. Earn the dough she's given me, and then fuck off.'

Famous last words.

7

The following Monday morning I decided to start with Nancy's tame copper, DI Bell, who I'd never come across before, and I hoped the experience was mutual. If it hadn't been for him I wouldn't have known where to begin, all my contacts on the force being dead, retired or of the opinion that I was somewhere south of a snake's belly on the professional front.

I put in a call to Fulham Police Station around ten-thirty.

'DI Bell,' I said to the male voice that answered the phone.

There was a click and a gruff voice said: 'Bell.'

'Morning, Inspector,' I said. 'My name's Sharman. I'm a private enquiry agent working for Nancy Stonehouse.'

There was a pause that seemed to stretch the length of the Fulham Road, if not all the way into Knightsbridge.

'Not *Nick* Sharman,' he said eventually.

Obviously he *had* heard of me.

'That's right.'

'Is this some sort of a joke?'

'I don't think so.'

'Why would Nancy Stonehouse hire you?'

'We're old friends. I was a friend of Harry's too.'

'Christ. This is all I need.'

A most auspicious start.

'I wondered if we might meet.'

31

'Keep on wondering.'

'I'm only trying to do my job.'

'Which is?'

'Finding out what happened to Harry during the year he was missing.'

'And what do you think I'm doing? Making daisy chains to earn my money?'

'No.'

'Then what?'

'I believe you're trying to find out who killed him.'

'Very good, Sharman. We'll make a copper of you yet. And I suppose you might have noticed that there could be some common thread between his disappearance and his death?'

'Sure. But I don't want to get involved in the murder.'

'Don't you? Well, I'm amazed. I thought murder was your business.'

'Not really.'

'Don't piss about, Sharman,' he said. 'I don't know what's going on here, but I intend to find out.'

'It's simple—'

'Sez you,' he interrupted. 'I'm going to speak to Mrs Stonehouse. You got a number there?'

I gave it to him.

'I'll call you back. And one thing. Don't step on my toes, son, or you'll wish you hadn't.' And with that he slammed the phone down.

I sat holding the dead instrument for a moment, then replaced it carefully on its base and lit a cigarette.

Next I tried 4F. The managing director's name was David Sutton, and he was in a meeting. So was his assistant. And his assistant's assistant probably, but I didn't ask. I told whoever I was talking to that I'd call back.

Productive morning so far.

The phone rang about five minutes later. It was Nancy.

'I've just had Philip Bell on the phone. He's furious.'

'Tell me something I don't know. I had a little chat with him myself, earlier.'

'He wants you off the case.'

'I'm not surprised.'

'I told him I wanted you to carry on.'

'What did he say to that?'

'Not a lot.'

'And?'

'And he hung up on me.'

'Me too. I hope he's watching his blood pressure.'

'You won't stop, Nick, will you?'

'I haven't properly started yet.'

'But you'll carry on.'

'I took your money.'

'Thanks. When are we going to get together?'

I could almost hear her nylons rasping together over the phone. 'Name a day.'

'Tomorrow. Dinner. Seven o'clock.'

'Sounds good. Just one thing. I don't have your address.'

She gave it to me and I jotted it down. Then we made our farewells and I put down the phone. It rang immediately. It was Bell.

'Seems like you're well in there,' he said.

'Look, I—'

He didn't let me finish. 'Just keep out of my way and you'll be all right,' he barked. 'Otherwise you're in deep shit,' and he hung up again.

So much for co-operation.

I tried 4F again and got through to David Sutton's assistant fresh from the meeting.

I went through the preamble, and enquired if I could come over and see Sutton.

'His book's pretty full,' said the assistant. A female. Once upon a time she would probably have been called his secretary.

'It won't take long.'

'Tomorrow at four?'

'Suits me.'

And that was how it started.

8

At four o'clock precisely the next afternoon I presented myself, all washed and neatly combed, at the glass and concrete palace hidden discreetly away behind a small wood on the edge of the residential area of Putney that housed the offices of 4F Security Inc.

David Sutton sat behind a desk made from a solid slab of black timber that looked as if it might support a small motor car, but held nothing heavier than a single telephone. A red one, of course.

He jumped to his feet at my entrance, and as his assistant closed the door discreetly behind me he danced across the expensive Wilton with his hand outstretched. He was wearing a smooth little grey worsted number that probably cost somewhere in the region of a grand and a half, over a pink and black striped shirt, and a tie that told me his political views were somewhere to the right of my own.

'Mr Sharman,' he said in an Eton and Oxford bray. 'I'm so sorry to have kept you waiting. I had no idea when you made the appointment that you were a friend of Nancy's. And Harry's, of course,' he added. 'But Nancy was on the blower a while ago and explained everything.'

'Good,' I said.

'Coffee? A drink?'

'Coffee would be fine.'

He hit the phone, barked an order and dropped it back on its rest.

'Do sit down,' he said, and I perched myself on an uncomfortable-looking leather and chrome affair in front of his desk.

'So how can I help? I've spoken to the police . . . A tragic affair.' He shook his head sadly, but not enough to disturb his mane of silver-grey hair.

'What happened to make Harry do a runner a year ago?' I asked bluntly.

He looked at me in wide-eyed innocence and said, 'God knows.'

'You must have some idea.'

'Believe me, I've racked my brains, both at the time and latterly when the tragedy of his death came to light. It was a dreadful shock to all of us here. He's sadly missed.'

'There must have been something.'

'I can only put his vanishing down to the stress of the job. Harry was high profile.'

'But he was a copper for a long time. He was used to stress. And that doesn't explain how come he ended up the way he did. Even the most stressed of us can hardly slice and dice our bodies up and leave the bits all over the place.'

I don't think Sutton was impressed by my logic. 'As you so rightly put it, Mr Sharman, Harry was a police officer for a long time. Perhaps his past caught up with him.'

'Perhaps,' I said. 'But let's get back to his disappearance. Tell me about the stress he was under.'

'Quite simply, the buck stopped with him here.'

'In what way?'

'For instance, if we had a loss.'

'Like a robbery?'

'Exactly.'

'Like the hijacking of that truck a couple of years ago?'

Sutton's face fell. The truck in question had held something close to twenty million quid in used notes due for the shredder. *En route* to its destination, a seemingly genuine message came over the truck's radio. The police had got a whisper that the truck was going to be hijacked. The driver was to make a detour, meet up with a police escort and proceed back to base. The meet was on an industrial estate just off the A3. On arrival the driver saw a squad car with two uniformed coppers and a plain saloon parked up. Reassured, the guard riding next to the driver got out to get instructions, the waiting men all produced semi-automatic weapons, the guard was grabbed by one of the fake coppers, doused in petrol and a box of matches was rattled by his ear. The driver took off in reverse but was boxed in by a third car, and when he tried to contact 4F on his radio he discovered that his transmission was being jammed. When one of the matches was lit next to his oppo's face, the driver surrendered. The guard in the back of the truck held out for another minute or two, but when he heard the hysterical voice of the driver over the intercom pleading for him to give in and save their mate's life, he opened the back up. The transfer of the money to the two unmarked cars and another van took just a few minutes, and the robbery was all over within five of the truck arriving.

At the time, it was the biggest cash snatch in British history, and went down with the Great Train Robbery in record books.

It took the police over six months to crack the case and start to make arrests. Eventually eleven people in this country were arrested and convicted, and a further eight warrants were still outstanding for fugitives, most of whom had been traced to Spain.

At the time of my meeting with Sutton, not one penny of the money had been recovered, and whoever had masterminded the affair, including getting the frequency of the radio in the trucks, which was changed twice a day, had never been caught.

'We don't like to talk about that one too much,' Sutton said.

I just bet you don't, I thought.

'Thank God we were well insured,' he continued.

'It wasn't like having the video nicked, though, was it?' I said.

'All our customers were recompensed.' He was up on his high horse now, and I thought it was time he was knocked off it.

'But it wouldn't have done your reputation much good.'

'No good at all.'

'And was Harry involved at the time?'

'Of course.'

'So that's the sort of stress you're talking about?'

'Correct.'

His assistant interrupted us with the coffee.

Whilst she poured it out I admired the view from the window, and the way her bottom filled out her tight skirt, and the perfect way that Sutton's distinguished grey hair curled over his collar.

When she had left us I said, 'So was Harry showing any particular signs of stress before he went?'

'No, he seemed fine.'

'So it's a complete mystery?'

'Completely.'

'I've tried talking to the police, Mr Sutton,' I said. 'But I'm not getting much co-operation. Have they come up with any theories about where he was for the year he went missing, do you know?'

'I've spoken to DI Bell who is in charge of the investigation locally,' said Sutton. 'We happen to belong to the same lodge.'

That explained a lot. I wondered why he hadn't given me the funny handshake, but then even washed and neatly combed I don't look like Mason material.

'But I'm afraid they're as baffled as the rest of us,' he said.

For some reason, and I don't know exactly what, I didn't entirely believe him.

'Is that so,' I said.

Sutton nodded, sipped his coffee and patted his lips dry with a pristine white handkerchief that he pulled from his sleeve.

I knew I was wasting my time, so I swallowed the remains of my drink and stood up. 'Well, thank you for your help,' I said.

Sutton waved his hand as if it had been nothing, and it had. 'Don't mention it,' he said as he rose too. 'If there's anything I can do to help Nancy, I will.'

I bet, I thought.

He came round and shook my hand again, and his grip was damp, but then it was a warm day, although the air conditioning in the building was on.

'Any time I can do anything,' he said too profusely, as he took my elbow and guided me to the door. 'Any time at all, just get in touch.'

'I will,' I said as he opened the door and slid me through the gap so gallantly that I almost expected him to blow me a kiss.

9

I was early for my dinner date, so I pointed the car north over Putney Bridge and went and scoped out Nancy's gaff. Forewarned is forearmed.

I was impressed. Well impressed. It was in a tree-lined street between the Fulham Road and the New King's Road. The house was double-fronted. A rarity round there, with a twin garage attached, small grounds and a short gravel-covered driveway up to the garage, which was reached through iron gates set in high walls. All in all, a right little *pied-à-terre*, and worth something in the region of three quarters of a million, I reckoned.

Obviously life *chez* Stonehouse wasn't exactly lived at subsistence level.

I drove off and found a boozer on the Fulham Road. It was called the Cat & Canary, part of a chain. But it was big and quiet at that time of night, and it served beer, so I didn't complain. I bought an evening paper and read it over a couple of pints and five Silk Cut.

At twenty to seven I left, and in the gathering dusk drove back to Nancy's.

I parked the car on the street and crunched up the gravel holding a bottle of decent red I'd bought in the local off-licence in one hand, and a bunch of sorry-looking flowers I'd purchased from the stall in front of the off-licence in the other.

I rang the bell and Nancy answered in a jiffy.

40

She was dolled up like a dog's breakfast in a short little clingy dark blue number which suggested mourning but didn't confirm it, black, sheer nylons, dark blue high heels, a Revlon counter of make-up, and she'd curled her hair into thick ringlets. She was holding a cigarette in one hand, and a half-full wine glass in the other.

The Merry Widow writ large.

I offered the wine and the flowers, she accepted both cheerfully, kissed me on the cheek, leaving a red lip mark that I saw in the hall mirror, and invited me in.

The hall itself was wide, sufficiently lit and opulent, with thick, patterned carpet on the floor, and a host of paintings on the walls. If even ten per cent were originals, Sotheby's would be drooling.

'Come on through,' she said, and did a sharp left through an arch into the living room.

That was rather less sufficiently lit, but just as opulent. The curtains were drawn and Barry White was on the stereo.

I figured I'd better keep my jock-strap buttoned or I could lose my honour.

'Sit down,' she said. 'Drink?'

'Sure.'

'Red or white?'

'Whatever you're having,' I said, nodding at her glass.

'Wise move.'

She left the room in the direction of, I assumed, the kitchen, which I must confess was oozing good smells, and returned a minute later with a goblet of wine for me.

I accepted it and lit a cigarette. 'So. What news?' she asked.

'You know the reaction I got from Bell. I got the bum's

rush at 4F too. Sutton was the soul of charm, but told me sweet FA. And he fancies you, by the way.'

'Tell me something new,' said Nancy, perching on the arm of my chair. 'He was always trying to grope me in the old days.'

She smelled good too, and I wished she'd find a chair of her own, when she said, 'S'cuse me, I've got to check the roast. You like lamb, I hope.'

'Definitely my favourite,' I said.

'With new potatoes, fresh peas, baby carrots, mint sauce and a very rich gravy.'

'Sounds too good to be true.'

'And my own apple pie to follow. It was a toss-up between that and some poncy *nouvelle cuisine*. But I remembered that you liked your meat rare and bloody.'

I'd heard it put more delicately, but it was true.

'You got me,' I said. 'Guilty as charged.'

She sloped off again, and I got up and checked the bookshelves. A lot of biography. Political. Kenneth Clarke, Michael Foot, Churchill. A smattering of hardback pop fiction in the Jilly Cooper mould. Some airport fodder paperbacks, some true crime, and a load about antique furniture. I checked the bureau next to the bookcase. It looked like it should be Chippendale. If it wasn't, then I was fooled. But I'm no expert.

Just then Nancy came back into the room and rescued her glass.

'Nice place,' I said. 'Quite a palace.'

'Harry picked it up cheap when he left the force. I oversaw the building work to bring it up to scratch, and chose the furnishings. I found I had the knack for picking up decent pieces for next to nothing. I discovered a talent I never knew I had.'

'Hence the books,' I said.

'That's right. It's been an education.'

'A profitable one, by the looks of it,' I said.

'Not really. I just pick pieces I like. Sometimes I sell them on, but I find I become too attached to part with them mostly. Come on through. We're eating in the kitchen. I hope you don't mind. If we used the dining room I'd have to keep vanishing.'

'You should see where I eat,' I said. Then I remembered she had, once upon a time.

She led me through to the kitchen which was about half the size of the Albert Hall, with a long, varnished table at one end by a set of French windows.

'Cosy,' I said. 'You could get my flat into here twice.'

'Does that bother you?'

'No.'

'Good.'

She sat me on one side of the table and her place was set on the other. She put a cute little apron over her dress and served the food.

It was great. The lamb was pink, tender and tasty, the vegetables were crisp, the mint sauce was home made, and the gravy reeked of booze.

The apple pie and cream that followed was great too, and she made coffee, and we went back into the living room. She perched on the edge of one of the armchair cushions, and I took the other.

Brandy and glasses were already set out on the coffee table and she said, 'Will you be mum?'

I grinned.

'What?' she said.

'That always makes me laugh.'

'I'm glad I still can.'

43

'Me too.'

After that we sat and shot the shit like old friends. The coffee pot and brandy bottle diminished rapidly, and Barry White became Simply Red, then Chris de Burgh, then Chris Rea. You can't be arrested for poor musical taste.

We hardly talked about Harry at all, and neither of us made a pass at the other. When I'd OD'd on soft rock, I looked at my watch. It was midnight and I was pissed.

'I'd better go,' I said.

'Do you have to?'

'I'm on the case, and I should do some work tomorrow.'

'Well, if you must.'

'I must,' I said. We shook hands at the door which was quite amusing, and I walked down the drive, fumbling for my car keys.

As I reached the street and made for the car a voice said, 'Not driving I hope, Sharman.'

I stopped dead and peered around. Sitting on the bonnet of a dark coloured, late-model Montego was a man. I thought I recognized the voice. I hoped I was wrong.

He pushed himself away from the motor and sauntered over. Then I knew that my fears were grounded.

'Remember me?' he asked.

As if I could ever forget. DS Jackson from Denmark Hill nick.

'You're a long way from home,' I said.

'Always ready to help a colleague,' he said in that arsehole accent of his. 'That your car?'

He pointed to mine.

'Yeah,' I said.

'Driving home?'

I shrugged.

'Looks like a set of car keys in your hand to me,' he said,

then changed the subject. 'See that car over there?' he raised his hand and headlights blinked. 'That's a traffic patrol with a couple of constables inside who'd be pleased to breathalyze you the minute you step inside your vehicle.'

'See that car there?' he asked, pointing back at the Montego. 'That's *my* car, and I'll be happy to give you a lift to the local nick in it to see my mate Philip Bell, and we can all have a nice chat over a cuppa.'

'You lot are closer than maggots in a tin,' I said.

'I'll pretend I didn't hear that,' said Jackson. 'So don't even think about driving, my son, otherwise you're up shit creek.'

'Thanks for the warning,' I said. 'Why didn't you just nick me?'

'Because you're a sensible man, Sharman, and we don't bear grudges. Leave Nancy and her problems to us. There's a dear.'

'I have a choice?'

'No. Stick your beak in and we'll chop it off. Now go back and do whatever you two do together, and get off the case.'

'Your word is my command,' I said, and I turned and walked back the way I'd come.

10

I went back up the drive and knocked on the front door. Nancy opened it on the chain. 'Forget something?' she said as she slipped the chain and opened the door all the way.

'There's two car-loads of Old Bill in the street. They've decided I'm a danger to public safety behind the wheel. Can I call a cab?'

'Come in,' she said.

I walked back into the warm hall and she said, 'How did they know you were here?'

'Christ knows. It's all down to your mate Bell. But at least it shows I must be doing something right.'

Nancy pulled a face. 'I'm making more coffee. Want some?'

'Can I use your phone first?'

'Oh, don't be silly Nick. That means you'll have to waste half the morning coming back for your car. There's three spare bedrooms upstairs. Stay over.'

I juggled the thought for a second, then said, 'OK. And I'll take that coffee too.'

After another two cigarettes and a cup of coffee, Nancy showed me to my room. It was at the back of the house, large and luxurious, with an en-suite shower room and lavatory, and the king-size bed was made up.

She left me alone and I cleaned my teeth with a new brush and paste I found in the bathroom cabinet, took a piss and climbed into bed. The sheets were crisp and cool

46

against my skin, the room was pitch dark, and I soon drifted into sleep.

What time she came into the room I don't know. It was still full night outside so it must've been early. She was warm and slippery and we did a lot of the things we'd done so long ago, and after she left I realized neither of us had said a word.

I fell asleep again and dreamed.

I dreamed about my second wife Dawn, and her friend Tracey, and my second daughter who would have been called Daisy if she'd ever been born and christened.

But she hadn't. She was consumed by the same fire that killed Dawn and Tracey early one morning on a deserted motorway.

All three had been murdered.

Then the dream changed and I was walking through a killing ground, a fully automatic machine pistol burning my hands as it pumped out its lethal load.

The air was full of a mist of blood, the stink of used gunpowder and the screams of the dying.

Then I saw her, as I always do when this particular dream chooses to haunt me. The girl in the white dress which blooms suddenly red, like a flower opening in the sun, and the look of surprise on her face as her faculties desert her and she falls to the floor.

A girl with a life that I stole. An innocent victim of a web of lies that I swallowed whole.

Then, thankfully, the dream changed again. I am sitting in a car on a lonely airfield. I hear the engines of a plane and see my hand reach for the gear stick and put it into low drive, and my foot goes down hard on the gas. I see the plane filling the windscreen and I see myself jam a briefcase full of money against the accelerator, wrestle open the car door and hurl myself on to the tarmac and watch as the car and plane meet in a terrible conflagration that destroys them both. As I lie there on the cold, hard ground watching burning money floating down from the sky after the explosion I see a man walk out from the flames, seemingly unhurt and coming towards me. I am unarmed and I know that he will kill me if he reaches me, but before he can he stumbles and falls flat on his face.

After minutes that seem like hours I drag myself towards him. He is my age and build and wearing a leather jacket, jeans and boots like mine. I remember that he was the pilot of the aircraft. He is dead, and I leave him and crawl off into the darkness.

I walk across country, through freezing streams and damp woods until it gets light. I shiver from the cold but keep walking for hours until I finally find a pub at a crossroads near a tiny village, clean myself up as best I can and go inside. No one takes much notice, as if a filthy stranger alone on foot in the deep, dark midwinter is hardly worthy of note.

And that's more or less where it stops. More drinks, a taxi, a coach maybe. Then London and my flat.

It all happened, just like the dream. Take my word. Only it was worse.

I woke up in a tangle of damp sheets with Nancy standing over me holding a steaming cup of tea.

11

She was wrapped up in a thick towelling robe, her face was scrubbed clean, and she looked to be about fourteen years old.

'Bad dreams?' she said.

I took the tea from her and had a sip. 'You tell me.'

'I've had worse.'

She didn't try and get back into bed and I didn't invite her. If she had, or I had, and she'd accepted, I think it would have finished that morning. Instead she said, 'It's half-eight. There's some bacon under the grill. How do you like your eggs? Over easy, isn't it?'

'You remembered,' I said.

'I'm like an elephant. I never forget. Five minutes,' and she turned and left.

I finished my tea, got up, went to the bathroom, got dressed and went downstairs.

The egg and bacon, tomatoes and toast were great. We sat together in the kitchen whilst we ate. We didn't talk about what had happened the previous night. We didn't talk about Harry. We didn't talk about much really. At nine-thirty I went back to the car, promising to call her if anything occurred. She kissed me on the cheek when I left. She smelled good.

I went home for a shave and a clean shirt, then toddled on down to the office. All was quiet and I sat and drank another cup of tea and had a think.

I thought about what had happened the night before, and the dreams I'd had, and what led up to them. Some of the thoughts were pleasant. Some weren't.

Then I had an unexpected visitor.

It was almost eleven by then and I was wondering about popping over to the boozer for a livener when my office door opened.

I looked up. 'Christ,' I said. 'Where did you spring from?'

'Victoria bloody Station. Where do you think?' said ex-Detective Inspector Jack Robber as he moved his bulk from the doorway to my client's seat, knocking the last couple of days' papers off it as he went. 'And then a bloody number two bus here.'

I looked at him. He appeared to have cleaned up his act since his retirement and move down to Worthing to live with his sister. He'd lost weight and his eyes were clear and bright. The greasy old mac was gone, replaced by a dark overcoat. His shirt collar was pristine, his tie unsullied by gravy and egg stains, his trousers neatly pressed, and his black shoes polished.

'I hardly recognized you, Robber,' I said. 'You look like you should be in Littlewoods' catalogue modelling natty gent's wear for the more mature man.'

He touched a nicotine-stained free hand to his neatly barbered hair, then ran it over his freshly shaven chin.

'It's bloody murder, Sharman,' he said. 'Living down there. I feel like a right prat in this get-up.'

'What's the matter?'

'It's that sister of mine. Glynis. I mean, she's the salt of the earth. But every time I take off a shirt it's in the bloody wash. And all she'll feed me is bloody rabbit food, and she puts bloody half fat milk in my tea. I'm only allowed a couple of pints a day, and there's no smoking in the house.' As if on cue he produced a packet of Benson's from the pocket of his coat and lit one.

'I'll smoke my own,' I said. At least his famous reputation for meanness with his fags was the same.

I lit up a Silk Cut and regarded him through the smoke. 'No more pork pies, then, Jack,' I said.

'Don't. I have to pretend to be taking the bloody dog for a walk to get one of them. She even made me salad sandwiches for the train.'

I had to laugh, and he scowled back at me.

'What's so bloody funny?' he demanded.

'You are,' I replied. 'Old bad, fat Jack Robber, the scourge of the south London villianati gone health conscious and skinny.'

He scowled some more. 'Not so much of the bloody "old".'

I held up one hand, thumb down. 'What's it like under there, Jack? All hot and sweaty, is it?'

He ignored my remark. 'She says it's for my own good. Her old man was a copper. He retired and dropped dead a month later.'

'That's the job,' I said.

He thought about that one, then said, 'For Christ's sake, let's go for a drink.'

We adjourned to the pub opposite and I bought us each a pint. His bitter, mine lager.

When we were seated at a table he said, 'I hear you're looking into Harry Stonehouse's murder.'

I stopped dead, my lager half-way to my mouth.

'How the fuck do you know about that?'

'I've still got my sources and contacts. Worthing isn't on the moon, you know.'

51

'Still . . .'

'I knew him,' said Robber.

'What did you think?'

'He was all right. Took the right courses, licked the right arseholes.'

'He retired early and got a good job.'

'S'right. Just what you'd expect really. His career wasn't fast track enough for him in the Met.'

'Straight?'

'Pretty much.'

'Meaning?'

'Meaning that any copper in this town has to look the other way sometimes.'

'Who told you, Jack? About me working on the case, I mean.'

He grinned evilly, just like the Robber of old. 'Later,' he said.

'So what exactly are you doing here today?'

'I hear that you're not getting much help from the constabulary. I'm going radio rental down by the seaside. I reckoned you could use a little help.'

'You want to work for me?'

'Bollocks, do I. I'll give you a hand. We split any money you make fifty-fifty. Stonehouse's missus isn't short, so I hear. How much has she paid you so far?'

'Later,' I said, with a grin of my own. 'This'll take a bit of getting used to. Know a copper called Philip Bell? DI at Fulham.'

''Course I do. Little shit. He's in charge, I believe.'

I nodded.

'You'll get nothing there.'

'And DS Jackson's in on the plot.'

'That fucker. He never did like you, did he?'

'I stepped on his favourite corns once or twice.'

'You want to be careful where you step. There's a lot of shit about. Shit that sticks.'

'I've had my share, Jack.'

'Don't I know it. So do you want me to help or not, or are you considering just sitting around your office until some likely lad comes along with a saw and a bundle of black plastic sacks and confesses? Because with all the help you'll be getting from our ex-colleagues, that's what'll have to happen for you to have any chance of getting to the bottom of this little lot.'

Straight to the point. And perfectly correct.

'But me, I've still got mates in the job, and I might be able to shake something loose,' he went on.

He knew he had me. 'Are you thinking about commuting to and fro from Worthing every day then, Jack?'

'Will I bollocks. I told you I'd still got contacts. There's a little widow keeps a nice clean boarding house on Knight's Hill. She's got a room going spare. B&B, use of phone, and something hot on the kitchen table at night if I want.'

'The mind boggles,' I said.

'So?'

'Sounds OK,' I said.

'So how much did she pay you?'

'You think I couldn't be doing this for love?'

'I doubt it, though I did hear something once . . .' He let the words hang for a moment. 'Just as well Harry didn't,' he added.

'A grand,' I said, changing the subject.

'Give us a monkey, then.'

The thousand quid had been burning a hole in my pocket since Nancy had come into the office, and I was almost relieved to peel off five hundred and slip it under the table into Robber's hand.

'So,' I said. 'What now?'

'What now is that I'll go and get my digs sorted. I'll do a little sniffing around then. Put myself about a bit. I fancy a decent ruby for a change. Meet me in the Star of India in Herne Hill at eight tonight and I'll bring you up to speed.'

'Whose treat will that be, then?' I asked.

'Whose do you fucking think?'

And that was how Jack Robber became my partner.

12

I was on time getting to the restaurant. Robber was late. Obviously I was more interested in hearing what he had to say than he was in saying it.

The place was pretty empty and I got a table for four at the back, and got stuck into a pint of Kingfisher and a couple of poppadoms and the condiment tray.

I was just coating a quarter of one of the giant crisps with a mixture of chutney, onion, tomato, and mint yogurt when he rolled in.

He saw me, came over, dropped into the seat opposite me and called for a pint of his own.

'Settled in, Jack?' I asked through a mouthful of food.

'That's right.'

'The little widow glad to see you?'

'Delighted.'

'Good. Now maybe you can earn the money I've paid you and tell me what you know.'

'Can't I get my drink in and order first?'

When his pint was in front of him and he'd gone through the curry card without referring to the menu, and I'd double ordered a couple of his choices, he sat back and looked at me.

'Right,' he said. 'What do you want to know?'

'Everything. Starting with who told you that Nancy had hired me.'

'Know a bloke called John Hague?'

I thought about it. 'Don't think so,' I said.

'Super on the murder squad. He's investigating Harry's killing.'

'What about Bell?'

Robber shook his head. 'Local. He came in when Harry disappeared last year. He's just holding Fancy Nancy's hand. Or anything else he can get hold of. Unless of course you've beat him to it.'

I ignored his remark.

'How come you got involved?'

'John's an old mate. We talk. Naturally, as soon as I read about Harry I got in touch. Then he phoned me yesterday, to tell me that Bell's got a bee in his bonnet because some tosser of a private detective's sniffing about the ground. When I heard it was you I nearly bust a gut.'

'And you came straight up. What a pal.'

Just then the steaming platters of food started arriving from the kitchen and pretty soon the whole table was full of them.

'She *must* be starving you,' I remarked as Robber piled up his plate and dived in.

'Nothing like a south London curry,' he said. 'They do try down by the seaside, but it ain't the same.'

'Must be the ambience of this place,' I said dryly, looking round the shabby interior of the restaurant.

'Dunno,' he said.

'So come on,' I said. 'What's cooking? Apart from the chicken dansak.'

Robber finished his first plate of food in record time and went round for seconds before he spoke.

'Right. Let's look at it logically.' He pulled an old envelope from his pocket. There was a spidery scrawl on the back.

'Last October, Harry Stonehouse, who had a good job, a lovely house, a flashy car and an equally flashy wife goes missing. The police are called in but come up against a blank wall.'

'And don't seem too interested.'

'According to Nancy. Right?'

I nodded.

'But according to John Hague on the other hand, DI Bell and his associates did a thorough-going job. It's not illegal to do a runner, you know. Harry left no criminal charges, no debts, no young birds with a bun in the oven or anything embarrassing like that.'

'Hague had to say that,' I said. 'He won't badmouth Bell. You know how the ranks close up.'

'He would to me. He knows what I think of Bell.'

I left that one. 'So was there another woman? One he went to, maybe? Nancy says no.'

'She would, wouldn't she? But I think she's right. There's no evidence that he set up a love nest in Paddington or anywhere, and he never touched a penny in any of his bank accounts.'

'Was there one no one knew about?'

'Could be. But once again Nancy told Bell that all monies were accounted for.'

'And he left his passport and papers and his beloved car behind.'

'Passports are easy, Nick. You know that.'

It was Nick now. The spicy food and beer was mellowing him out.

'So it's a mystery?'

'But a good one. More about that later.'

He referred to the envelope again. 'Now two months ago our Harry starts turning up like a bad penny all over town.' He thought for a moment. 'Shocking,' he said. 'With a year missing out of his life.'

'So where was he, and are there any suspects in the murder case?'

'You want me to do everything, don't you?' said Robber, spearing a succulent piece of king prawn off my plate.

'You copped a monkey this morning, Jack,' I said. 'So far I think I could've told you what you've just told me. And I have to ask myself if you're worth it.'

He grinned through gappy teeth and said, 'Ah. But now it gets interesting.'

'How?'

'I phoned up Johnny Hague again today. Told him where I was, and what I was doing, and he shtummed up.'

'More toes being trod on.'

'I don't think so.' He wiped his plate clean with nan bread and loaded it up for a third time. I'd had enough and pushed my plate away and lit a cigarette.

'Come on, then,' I said. 'Don't keep me in suspense.'

He took a small piece of something from his mouth, looked at it suspiciously, put it on the side of his plate, chewed, then swallowed, took a mouthful of lager, swallowed that too, and said, 'Johnny didn't seem to mind me looking into Harry's murder. But when I told him we were investigating the lost year he suddenly found he had another engagement.'

'So?'

'So, you're not using your loaf, Sharman. I reckon he knows exactly where Harry Stonehouse was for that year, and exactly who killed him.'

13

I dogged out my cigarette and waved the waiter over. I ordered two Irish coffees, and when the waiter had gone I said, 'And what makes you jump to that stunning conclusion so soon into the investigation?'

'I've been doing my homework. Earning that monkey you gave me this morning. And by the way I think it's about time you billed the lady and got some more dough. And I bought you this.' He fumbled in his overcoat pocket and pulled out a tiny portable phone which he put on the table between us. 'It's on line. The number's here. And all the instructions.' He went back into his coat, pulled out a small handbook and gave it to me. 'Sixty minutes free airtime a month. I've got one too. Cheap and cheerful. I've missed mine since I left the force. I'll take cash. No kites.'

'A portable fucking phone,' I said, poking it gingerly with my finger.

'Get into the nineties, son,' he said. 'We need to keep in touch.'

'And you expect me to pay for both of them?'

'You've got the other monkey. I'll get the dough in the morning. Now put it away, you'll have people thinking you're a yuppie.'

'I thought they were all dead.'

'Exactly.'

I picked up the phone and put it in my pocket and said, 'So. Homework? Tell me about it.'

'You don't last as long in the job as I did without knowing where a few bodies are buried, and being owed a few favours. So I phoned a bloke I know at CRO and he went into the SID computer software for me—'

'What's that?' I interrupted.

'SID. Systems Intelligence bollocks of some kind. It's new.'

'And that's *SIB*.'

'Piss off.'

'Yeah? And?'

'And Harry Stonehouse was a target.'

'No.'

'I swear.'

'When?'

'Up until about a month before he disappeared.'

'Target for what?'

'The blag. The big 4F blag.'

'You're joking.'

'On my life.'

'Well fuck me,' I said. 'No wonder David Sutton got his knickers in a twist when I mentioned it.'

Robber looked puzzled and I told him what had happened when I'd visited 4F Security's offices the previous day.

'Thanks for telling me,' he said. 'Every little bit of information helps.'

'Seems like you're doing all right on your own,' I said. 'What do you reckon?'

'I reckon there's twenty million quid out there waiting for someone to claim it. What do you reckon, Sharman? Fancy a slice?'

14

'I reckon it's getting too bloody heavy for me. Twenty million quid. You get killed for that.'

'Tell Harry Stonehouse.'

'Shit. So where was he?'

'Ever heard of witness protection? It was just after he vanished that we started to pick up faces.'

'We?'

'I was in the job then.'

'So Harry got picked up, leant on, he grassed and vanished out of everyone's lives?'

'Looks like it to me.'

'And got a new identity? Hence leaving all his papers behind.'

'Top of the class.'

'But he got sussed.'

Robber nodded. 'It makes sense.'

'And his old mates topped him.'

Another nod.

'Didn't do a very good job, did they? The Old Bill who got him away.'

'That's the breaks.'

Something occurred to me. 'So just as a matter of interest, who was targeting him? Specific officers, I mean.'

'I wondered when you'd ask that. Who do you think, round Putney way?'

'Not DI Bell by any chance?'

'In one.'

'Cosy.'

'I'll say.'

'I wish I could've been a fly on the wall when Harry turned up dead.'

'I'll bet you do.'

'Not a good advert for Bell's office's security.'

'Not at all.'

'Beautiful. But hold on. If Harry *was* part of the robbery, and we don't even know for sure that he was, and all you're surmising is true, which ain't necessarily so, he could still've had some bird stashed away in a quiet corner, and maybe someone took exception. But even if what you say *is* true, and Harry gave up the whole gang in exchange for a new life. Why didn't he tell where the money was? He must've known.'

'Just what I was thinking, Sharman. Maybe it's time we put on our detective hats and found out.'

15

We sat in the restaurant for a bit longer, drinking more Irish coffees and discussing what might've been regarding Harry Stonehouse and the whereabouts of the missing millions.

'Did you have anything to do with the investigation at the time?' I asked Robber.

He shook his head. 'No. Not a thing. Well out of my manor, and I never heard a whisper concerning it.'

'Not even that Harry was in the frame?'

'Not a dicky bird.'

'Did you ever talk to him about it?'

'No. We weren't that great mates. Especially after he left the job.'

I looked at him through the smoke that wreathed our table. 'So this has been about the money all along. Not about your poor dead pal.'

Robber grinned nastily. 'You've got a suspicious mind, Sharman.'

'I need one with people like you about.'

'All right, I give in. When I spoke to Hague, he let it slip that there might be a connection.'

'So why all the old bollocks?'

'I didn't know how keen you'd be.'

'Not keen at all as it goes.'

'Exactly.'

'But Harry was always straight. I'd've staked my life on it.'

'Twenty million quid can be very persuasive.'

'It was going to be split about twenty ways the way I heard it.'

'And the geezers it was going to be split by could be very persuasive too.'

'Old-fashioned heavies, you mean.'

'Their last fling before it got too hot here and they split for Spain.'

'But Harry had mates still. On the force, I mean. He didn't have to cave in.'

'Your mates change when you leave the job. Old loyalties don't last too long out in the real world.'

'You make it sound depressing.'

'I forgot. You didn't have any mates, did you?'

'A few.'

'But they're all gone now, aren't they?'

'Except for you.'

'Now you're depressing me.'

'Cheers. So listen. Let's say we do look into this a little closer and Harry *was* involved, and by some miracle we come up with the money. What happens then?'

'I've always fancied seeing Trinidad and Tobago.'

'We keep it, you mean.'

'Top of the class, Sharman.'

'I don't like it.'

'What? Are you getting honest in your old age?'

'I've always been honest, underneath it all.'

'Sure. But it's a long way down.'

'Thanks. I thought we were partners.'

'We are, but it doesn't hurt to know exactly who your partners are.'

I lit a final cigarette and signalled for the bill. 'Right. Where do we start?'

'I'll go back to my contacts. You go back to Nancy. That won't be any hardship for you, will it?'

'OK, Jack, but I'm sure I'm going to live to regret this.'

'Maybe, maybe not. But if we have a result at least your lifestyle will improve.'

'Or I'll die in the attempt.'

'We've all got to die, Sharman. That's the only certainty.'

And on that happy note we left.

16

I drove Robber back to his widow's house in Knight's Hill, then headed home alone and arrived around midnight. I parked the old BMW I was driving on the space outside the house, locked it up and went inside.

I climbed the stairs to the top and put my key in the flat door and opened it. There was a light on inside. I hadn't left one on and I stiffened, then a voice with a slight lisp said from behind me, 'Go on in, Mr Sharman. We're all waiting.'

I turned slightly, heard the whistle of displaced air, my head seemed to explode into a thousand pieces and I was suddenly falling through the door and the pattern on the living room carpet got bigger and bigger.

I came to when someone washed my clock with the contents of a pint glass of cold water. I was sitting in my favourite chair which had been turned round from the TV set to face the centre of the room. Three men were standing looking at me.

They were perfect. The one on the right was a good-looking young Asian with thick black hair swept back in a quiff. He was wearing a silver suit probably from Armani with a black shirt buttoned to the neck, sans tie. On his feet he wore black leather casual shoes and his eyes were disguised by sunglasses. The one in the middle was short and built like a little steamroller who just couldn't wait to roll right over you. Or me probably in this case. He had

66

receding dark hair cut very short, which made his round face look even rounder, and was wearing a single-breasted black overcoat, black jeans, black polo neck and black Doc Marten's. He was holding the empty glass. The one on the left was Greek or Turkish with a thick mass of black curly hair going grey, and a moustache that made him resemble Groucho Marx. He wore a dark overcoat too. Double-breasted, and almost down to his ankles.

'Where did you lot come from?' I asked, wiping the water off my face. 'Central casting?'

'Very amusing,' said the steamroller. He didn't have a lisp, therefore he hadn't been the one who'd hit me on the head.

I suspected the Asian.

He spoke next. 'I hope you had a good evening, Mr Sharman.'

Lisp in place. I'd been right.

'Not bad,' I replied. 'The chicken was good, but I think the chef put too much chilli in the niramish. Relative of yours, by any chance?' I asked him. 'What is this, a customer survey?'

'What the fuck's he talking about?' said Groucho. I knew then and there we were going to get on.

'He's a funny fucker,' said Steamroller. 'I told you that already.'

'Do I know you?' I said to him.

'No. But I know *you*, son. You've got a big nose. Like your mate Robber.'

'Put you away, did he?' I said, then turned to the Asian, who although he was the youngest I took to be the leader. 'Mind if I smoke?'

'Go ahead,' he said. 'We don't want to make this harder than we have to.'

'As the actress said to the bishop,' I said as I took out my cigarettes.

Steamroller moved forward faster than seemed possible for someone carrying his bulk and knocked the packet out of my hand. 'Don't take the piss,' he said.

The Asian rescued the box and gave me a cigarette. 'Now, now, my friend,' he said to Steamroller. 'Let's not be unpleasant.'

And I suppose a whack on the nut is just your way of saying hello, I thought, but wisely kept my mouth shut and fired up my Silk Cut.

'We came to give you some advice, Mr Sharman,' said the younger man leaning against the wall. 'We don't want to make any trouble for you and your friend. Just stay out of what doesn't concern you and all will be well. Otherwise . . .' He didn't finish the sentence.

'But you made trouble for Harry Stonehouse,' I said. It had to be about Harry.

'Harry broke the rules of the road,' said the Asian. 'Don't you make the same mistake. Or next time . . .' Once again he left the words unspoken.

'And that's not a threat, it's a promise,' said Groucho. 'If it was up to me . . .'

'If it was up to him you'd end up in the same place as Harry Stonehouse,' said Steamroller. '*And* if it was up to me.'

'The same *places*,' said the Asian. 'But let's not dwell on such unpleasant subjects. We'll be going now. Just remember – you don't get a second warning.'

And one by one they left the room, went downstairs and I heard the front door close behind them, then the sound of a powerful engine starting and a car moving away.

I went to the window, but the street was deserted except for a ginger cat walking across the pavement in front of the house.

17

I took the piece of paper Robber had given me with the number of his portable phone on it, and used my ordinary phone to dial it. I hate portable phones and always said I'd never use one. But I suppose they do have their advantages.

He answered after two rings, sounding like I'd woken him.

'All alone?' I said.

'What the fuck—?'

'I've had visitors,' I interrupted. 'They left me a souvenir.'

'What?'

'A lump on the head,' I said, gently touching the back of my skull.

'Who were they?'

I described them. 'They knew you,' I said at the end. 'At least one of them, intimately.'

'Which one?'

'The steamroller bloke,' I replied.

'Geezers like him are ten a penny. I probably gave him a tug once.'

'If he gives you a tug now, I reckon you'll know all about it.'

'Scum like that don't scare me.'

'They scare me plenty. It's all about Harry Stonehouse.'

'That's good.'

'You reckon.'

''Course. It means we're going down the right road. The right road to lots of dough.'

'Or the cemetery. They told me what would happen if we didn't butt out.'

'What?'

'The same as Harry. A ride to the nearest tip inside garbage bags.'

'Nothing's for nothing, Sharman. Now go rest your head and we'll talk tomorrow. I'll meet you for breakfast in that greasy you like about nine.'

'Who's tab this time?'

'I'll treat you.'

'I'll make a note of it in my diary.'

'Do that.' And he hung up.

18

I woke up around eight with a headache and a lump the size of a hen's egg on my napper. I washed and shaved, got dressed and was at the café with a mug of tea, the *Telegraph* and a bacon sandwich on the way by the time Robber joined me.

'How's your head?' he asked after he'd ordered tea and a full English for himself.

'Sore,' I said.

'You should be more careful in your choice of friends.'

'Cheers.'

He made me go over everything the three geezers had said when they'd paid me a visit the previous night. 'I was bloody right,' he said when I'd finished. 'I knew it. I knew that bastard was bent.'

'Which doesn't actually do a lot for us,' I remarked.

'It will. When we've finished here, you go and see the lady in question and I'm going to take a wander round some of my old haunts. The widow said I could borrow her car when I want it.'

'Just be careful,' I said as my bacon sandwich was plonked in front of me, and Robber's plate got dropped in front of him. 'Those fuckers last night meant business. And you can't hide behind your warrant card any more. And your widow sounds like she means business too if she's letting you drive her motor. She'll have you in bed with her before you can say knife.'

He sneered at me as he poured brown sauce on to his egg. 'Don't worry about me, son. Just make sure you've got on clean underwear for Nancy's benefit.'

After breakfast we parted outside the café and I walked back up to collect my car, and Robber headed home to borrow his landlady's.

I called Nancy when I got in and told her I needed to see her, and she asked me round for morning coffee.

How civilised, I thought as I put down the phone and wondered if there'd be any fairy cakes.

I got to her place round eleven and she had Richard and Judy on the TV as she let me in. 'My secret vice,' she said as she hit the remote and turned them into a white dot when we went into the living room. 'They keep me company. But you're much better.'

'Thanks,' I said.

She was dolled up in a low-cut number in dark grey and I could smell her perfume clear across the room. She looked good. 'So what's happening?' she asked.

'Not a lot,' I lied. I didn't tell her about my nocturnal visitors or the fact that Robber was now working with me.

She served us coffee and biscuits on a tray, but sadly there was no sign of cake.

'Nancy,' I said when the coffee was finished and I'd lit a cigarette. 'Tell me about what happened before Harry disappeared.'

'Like what?' She looked puzzled.

'Anything. Anything unusual.'

'There wasn't anything.'

'There must've been. People don't just run away for no reason. There's always something. Debt. A love affair. Something at work, or something at home. Believe me, I know. There's always a reason, no matter how large or small.'

73

'Nick. I really don't have a clue. Like I keep telling you, we didn't talk much at the end.'

'Normally I'd say that that was it. If it hadn't gone on for so long and he hadn't been found in the condition that he was.'

'I told you I don't know.'

'You're not being much help, Nancy.'

'That's why I'm paying you to find out for me.'

And I wished that she wasn't. 'I know that,' I said. 'But it's the same old story. I'm just one bloke. If Old Bill can't come up with anything with all their resources, what chance do I have?'

'You seem to have done all right with your other cases.'

'Sometimes. But I need something to work with. People to talk to. So far I've come up with a big blank. What about these friends you talked about? Golfing buddies, whatever.'

'I knew some of them personally from the parties we used to have.' She came over all coy at that. 'And others just by name. They're all in his address book.'

'I'd better have that, I think. I'll talk to them. Maybe they'll know something you don't.'

'All right, Nick. I'll get it.' And she rose from her chair and left the room wafting a cloud of her exotic perfume behind her.

She came back a few moments later carrying a burgundy leather Filofax bulging with pages. 'He used this as a diary, too,' she said. 'I'd appreciate having it back.'

I riffled through a few of the address pages, which were packed with names and phone numbers in Harry's neat printing. It was kind of spooky to think that the man who'd written them was now dead.

'So, what now?' she asked.

'I'll look through the book and call some people up. I

74

expect I'll get told to take a hike by most of them, but you never know. I'll play the wide-eyed innocent and come up with some bullshit story or another.'

'It's been a long time since you've been a wide-eyed innocent.'

'Too bloody true.'

She shifted her legs and I knew what was coming next. 'You don't have time for lunch, do you?'

'What do you mean by lunch, Nancy?'

'You know. Maybe some cheese on toast and a beer and a fuck. Or possibly a fuck and then some cheese on toast and a beer.'

'I don't think that's a great idea.'

She pouted. 'I do.'

'Nancy, this is business.'

'That's not what you said the other night.'

'I don't think I said much the other night. You kind of took me by surprise.'

'Poor baby. Poor, wide-eyed innocent baby.'

'OK, Nancy, you got me. But that was a one-off, wasn't it?'

Obviously it wasn't. Maybe I was more of an innocent than anyone thought, including myself.

'It didn't have to be.' She was getting playful then, a mood I knew well and always seemed to end up the same way, with me and her in bed together.

'Listen, Nance,' I said almost pleadingly. 'You're paying me to work for you.'

'And what did you think you'd be doing? Lying on your back and counting spiders' webs on the ceiling?'

'Nancy, you're far too thorough a housekeeper to allow any spiders' webs in the place and you know it.'

'A figure of speech.'

'OK. But you know what I mean.'

'And you know what *I* mean.' Which took the conversation almost full circle.

And then my portable phone rang.

For a quarter of a minute I didn't know what the hell this strange warbling that came from my chest area was.

'I didn't know you had one of those,' said Nancy

'Shit, telephone,' I said, not knowing I had one myself for a moment. And I pulled it out of my inside coat pocket, flipped down the cover and said, 'Hello.'

'Robber,' said Robber. 'Where are you?'

'At Mrs Stonehouse's house.'

'You're so formal. Get dressed and get back over here. I'll meet you in the pub.' And he cut me off.

I looked at Nancy sadly. 'Sorry,' I said. 'Duty calls.'

'Another time, then,' she said, looking disappointed.

'We'll see.' And I put away the phone, picked up the Filofax, pecked Nancy on the cheek and left, feeling half-relieved and half-disappointed.

But that's human nature.

19

I assumed Robber meant the pub opposite my office, so I pointed the car back over the river and aimed it down the South Circular. It took me about thirty minutes to get there and I'd been right. Robber was waiting with his nose in a pint and a meat pie smeared with tomato ketchup and mustard half-eaten on a plate in front of him.

'Didn't you have enough breakfast?' I said as I joined him.

'Lunch,' he said. 'Want some? Or have you eaten?'

'Meaning?'

'Meaning you know what. What's between the lovely Nancy's thighs. Hair pie.'

'You're such a gent, Jack,' I said. 'But you're barking up the wrong tree. I'm going to get a drink.'

'Mine's a best bitter,' he said.

I got a bitter for him and a lager for myself and went back to the table. 'So what's up?' I asked.

'I put a few feelers out. The old pal's act. A name came up. One I know.'

'Who?'

'A snout. Not one of mine. Name of Norbert Green. Funny little bugger. Nervous Norbert, they used to call him.'

'What about him?'

'Well, apparently, according to this contact of mine—'

'Inside the force?' I interrupted.

'Correct. According to this contact of mine inside the force, Nervous Norbert has been putting it about that he knew something about Harry Stonehouse's demise.'

'And your contact has done nothing.'

'On the contrary. My contact pulled Nervous Norbert in for a chat.'

'And?'

'And Norbert denied all knowledge. But my contact is adamant that Norbert was telling another little shit who happens to be my contact's snout that he did know something.'

'So?'

'So Norbert was equally adamant that he doesn't.'

'Where did the original conversation take place between these two fine upstanding citizens. Nervous Norbert and this unnamed snout?'

'In a boozer. Late. A bit of afters.'

'And all the snouts were having a convention, were they? What's the pub called? The Green Green Grass of Home?'

Robber gave me a dirty look.

'So this is the big news,' I said. 'This is what you dragged me back here for?'

'Missing her, are you? And what have you got? Anything?'

'This,' I said, taking the Filofax from where it was dragging down the pocket of my jacket and dropping it on the table in front of him. 'It's Harry Stonehouse's.'

'And there's me thinking you'd gone all yuppified again. What with the portable phone first and now that.'

I ignored his snide comments. 'I thought we'd go through it,' I said. 'See if there's any names we recognized.'

'Good idea. But first I want a little chat with Norbert.'

'So chat to him.'

'I want you there too.'

'Why? I don't know the geezer.'

'Because as you so rightly said, I can't hide behind my warrant any more. And you have a certain look about you, Sharman.'

'What kind of look?'

'Something not nice. Something that says you'll hurt anyone who doesn't come across with what you want.'

'And there's me thinking I had a kind face.'

'Think again.'

'So where do we find Norbert?'

'He used to hang out in a pub called the Angel of Mercy.'

'Down Peckham Rye.'

'That's it.'

'Delightful. I've been there. A right cosy little place. They'd nick a blind man's guide dog in there for sandwich filling.'

'Then you should feel right at home. Drink up and we'll be going.'

20

We took Robber's motor down to the Rye. Or should I say his landlady's. It was a geriatric Sierra that smelled of cat's piss. 'Did Tiddles have an accident?' I said as we pulled away.

'She hasn't used it for a bit. It was in the garage with the window open. Some bleeding cat's been sleeping in it. Keep the window open and it doesn't notice.'

But even with all the windows down it did, and I lit a cigarette to mask the smell.

'She doesn't like smoking in the car.'

'I don't like cat's peeing in the car. Put up some notices.'

We parked in a supermarket car park opposite the boozer twenty minutes later and dodged through the traffic to the door of the saloon bar.

Inside it was dark and smoky with maybe half a dozen fruit machines on the go, the jukebox playing some techno crap and both pool tables in use at the back. There were about thirty people inside getting on the outside of pints. They were all men, and most looked to be just an inch from punching someone out. 'Great,' I said to Robber. 'It's just like I remembered it.'

We went to the bar and the geezer served us two pints. 'Norbert been in?' said Robber.

'Norbert who?'

'Norbert Green.'

'Who wants him?'

'An old friend.'

'Don't know him.'

'OK,' said Robber and we went to a vacant table littered with dirty glasses and a full ashtray and sat down.

'Discreet,' I said.

'He'll be here.'

An hour and two drinks later the door opened and a little geezer who looked like a bookie's runner came in. The barman brushed imaginary fluff off his shirt sleeve and the runner turned and left.

'That's him,' said Robber. 'Come on.'

We left our drinks and hit the street. I saw the back of the geezer turning into Woolworth's and Robber dived down a side street and I went into the shop after Green.

He cut through to the back entrance where Robber was waiting just slightly out of breath. 'Norbert,' he was saying as I went through the door after Green. 'What's the hurry?'

'You've got the wrong man,' said Norbert.

'Sure,' said Robber. 'And I'm the queen of the fairies.'

Norbert turned and I caught him by the arm. 'Don't be a stranger, Norbert,' I said. 'Let's get a drink.'

The bookie's runner looked petrified and Robber said, 'There's another boozer over there. Come on, I'll buy you a pint, Norbert.'

This I had to see, and flanking the little guy we went over the road into a pub called the Pit Pony, although in that area it would've been better called the Pit Bull.

As a matter of fact, inside it wasn't too bad, and Robber actually sprung for three drinks, and we took Norbert to a quiet table in a corner close to a dead open fire.

'You must remember me, Norbert,' said Robber when we were seated and all smoking my fags.

Norbert shook his head.

'I was afraid of that,' said Robber. 'I used to be a copper. Detective Inspector at Gypsy Hill.'

'Used to be,' said Norbert.

'I'm retired now.'

'So what do you want?' Norbert again.

'Harry Stonehouse. Name ring a bell?'

Norbert looked sick and went the colour of yesterday's rice pudding. He shook his head again.

'Don't piss about, son. Me and my pal here don't appreciate it.'

Norbert looked at me for the first time. I kept my gob zipped.

'I'm freelance now,' Robber went on. 'Me and him work together. He's an animal.'

I tried to adopt an animal persona, but I didn't know which one. A squirrel? A lion? An elephant?

Norbert's hand was trembling as he picked up his glass.

'See, Norbert,' said Robber. 'We have no rules now. No PACE. No tape recorders. We'll hurt you and enjoy doing it. You do believe me, don't you?'

Norbert nodded, and I knew we had him.

'So tell me about Harry Stonehouse. You were going on about him before, weren't you? Boasting, like.'

'I don't know nothing, Mr Robber,' said Norbert, and now he was shaking all over. Johnny Kidd and the Pirates. Shit. That was oldie but goodie.

'Bollocks, Norbert,' said Robber. 'We're getting tired of all this shit.' He nodded in my direction. 'You want him to take you out to the toilets and chop your balls off or what?'

Me, I thought. I'd no more touch Norbert's balls than walk barefoot through a vipers' nest, but I suppose he wasn't to know that. At least by the look of fear he gave me he didn't.

'No, Mr Robber.'

'So tell us.'

Norbert licked his lips. 'I know this bloke, he's a biker. A right nutter. Crazy Larry, they call him.'

Fuck, I thought. Do all these wankers have nicknames?

'He's in a gang. Street Shit they call themselves. SS for short. Anyway, he drinks in a boozer over in Croydon. The Deliverance.'

My heart sank. Street Shit. SS. Deliverance. Nightmare time, and I was awake.

'What about him?' said Robber.

'Listen,' said Norbert pleadingly. 'I'll be straight with you. I deal a little blow sometimes. Just as a sideline. I sell it to the gang amongst others. Christ, but they love coke, specially Larry. He's always trying to find out where my wholesaler is so that the gang can hit him. Anyway, one night we're all round his place having a little party, and we've done about five grams and he gets carried away and starts talking. He told me about this job him and the gang got. Getting rid of this bloke's body. They were supposed to take it out into the country and burn it. They got paid in coke. But what happened, see, was that they dipped into the product and got blitzed, so in the end all they did was chop him into bits and put him into garbage sacks and dump him wherever they could.'

'Harry Stonehouse,' interrupted Robber.

'It had to be. It was in the papers.'

'And who paid them?'

Norbert shrugged. 'Christ, I don't know. Before he got that far the others shut him up and that was that.'

'Good Norbert,' said Robber. 'Good boy.'

Norbert was as grateful as a whipped dog getting a pat on the head. 'Is that all?' he asked.

'Not quite. Where's this flat of his at?'

'On the New Addington estate. In a tower block. They took me there. I was pissed. I don't know the address.'

'That's not so good,' said Robber.

'But he's always in the pub Fridays.' Today was Thursday.

'Good,' said Robber. 'Excellent, in fact.'

'How will we recognize this geezer?' I asked, speaking for the first time since we'd come into the pub.

'You'll recognize him all right,' replied Norbert. 'They call him Crazy Larry because he said he could jump Tower Bridge on his bike when it was opening.'

I looked at Robber who said, 'Did he?'

Norbert nodded. 'But he came a right cropper. His bike hit the lip of the far side of the bridge and he came off. He lost his left hand, so now he wears a false one. It's painted red. So you'll know him right away.'

Fucking hell, I thought. Can this get any worse?

'Terrific,' I said.

'You won't mention my name, will you?' said Norbert.

''Course not,' said Robber. 'But, Norbert, I don't think you'd better tell anyone about this conversation. Especially Crazy Larry.'

'What conversation?' Norbert might not be the brightest individual in south London, but he'd been around the block enough times to know a serious threat when one was made, however obliquely. But he had to spoil it. 'Is it worth something?' he asked.

Robber smiled. 'Sure, Norbert,' he said. 'It's worth us not kicking your arse from here to Christmas. Now fuck off before we change our minds.'

Norbert got up and prepared to flee.

'And lay off the coke, son,' I said. 'Too much coke'll make you even more nervous.'

Norbert nodded and almost ran out of the pub.

21

Robber and I stayed in the pub with the remains of our drinks. 'I told you it would start to come together,' he said as he nicked another of my cigarettes.

'Mainly down to you, Jack,' I admitted. 'I'd never've come up with Norbert in a million years.'

'Perseverance, boy. But it makes me wonder why no one else has.'

'Bothered, you mean.'

'Exactly.'

'Funny, that.'

'We'll find out. How do you fancy a noggin in Croydon tomorrow night?'

'At the Deliverance.'

He nodded.

'With Crazy Larry with one red hand?'

Another nod.

'Wonderful. It'll make my weekend. Did you ever see that film?' I asked.

'What film?'

'*Deliverance.*'

'One of my favourites.'

'In-breeding. It's kind of like that in some parts of Croydon too.'

'But can anyone play the banjo?'

I laughed at that.

'Reckon they'll try and make us squeal like little piggies?' he asked after a moment.

'While they're giving it to us up the arse, you mean?'

He nodded again.

'They could try.'

'Got any handguns, Nick?'

I smiled. 'A couple.'

'Ammunition?'

'Gun's no good without bullets.'

'They legal?'

'Now what do you think?'

'Untraceable?'

'Hope so.'

'Maybe we'd better take one each. We might need some firepower to separate this Crazy Larry joker from the pack.'

'Suits me. I hate to go drinking unarmed.'

He grinned. 'You're a soppy fucker, Nick, you know that?'

'I try my best.'

'Let's go, then. I'll drop you off.'

'Cheers. If anyone needs me I'll be home cleaning my guns.'

22

When Robber dropped me off at the flat I went upstairs and opened up the little door I'd built into the crawl space under the roof and dug out the two handguns I kept there. One was a Browning 9mm BDA with a fourteen-shot magazine, and the other a six-shot Colt Detective Special revolver with rubber grips. The Colt used to belong to my wife before she was murdered and has great sentimental value. The niner I couldn't really care less about.

I took them, spare ammunition and extra magazines for the Browning down into my flat. My special bubbah, a Uzi carbine, neatly wrapped in clear plastic, I left behind. That one was for special occasions only.

I cleaned both weapons, loaded them and two of the extra Browning clips and stashed them away in the springs under the bed. Not the perfect place, but it would do unless an expert spun the place and knew what he or she was looking for.

That evening I had a date with Diane and I drove the Beemer up to town. We'd discovered a pub in Docklands a bit off the beaten track that wasn't too bad, and just down the road was a decent Thai restaurant.

I was on time and she was late. Pretty much par for the course. When she arrived I was about half-way through a pint and watching a boat chugging down the river that lapped at the outside wall of the pub. Broken cloud filled the sky and the rays of the setting sun splashed through it like the light was solid gold bars.

'Am I late?' she asked.

'No later than usual.'

'Want a drink?'

'Another pint, please.'

She went to the bar, and like ninety per cent of the other geezers in the bar I admired the way her body filled the light woollen, navy blue dress she was wearing. As I watched her I felt something slip through my fingers like quicksilver that I'd never be able to collect together again. It wasn't the first time I'd had that feeling, but I suspected that the times I'd feel it again were strictly numbered.

'How's the case going?' she asked when she sat down.

'Not bad.'

'And how's the lady?'

I felt we were heading into uncharted waters. Or maybe they were being charted as I sat there. 'Not bad,' I said again.

'Fucked her yet?'

'No,' I lied.

'Liar.'

'No,' I lied again.

'Liar.'

'Is it going to be one of those evenings?' I asked.

'What evenings?'

'When you ask me questions, I answer, you call me a liar and I deny it.'

'Could be.'

'Then there's no point.'

'To what?'

'To us being together.'

'Is that what you think?'

I looked at her, and thought how beautiful she was, and young, and I felt old and hopeless and the dying sun cut into my eyes and I knew that it was my whole life that was slipping away and I could do nothing about it.

23

Before I could answer, her face softened. 'Sorry, Nick,' she said. 'It's not a good time of the month for me.'

It's never a good time of the month for me I thought, but didn't say.

'Pain in the belly,' she said.

And the unspoken drift was that she didn't want me poking around her insides, which, although I thought I'd never live to see the day, was a bit of a relief. I was getting to like sleeping alone. Or at least if I couldn't sleep with Dawn, then I preferred being on my own.

'Do you want to go home?' I asked

She shook her head. 'I might as well be in pain here and take it out on you as at home alone. I haven't even got a cat to kick.'

That was more like the old Diane and we both smiled. 'Do you want to eat or what?' I said.

'In a bit. Tell me about the case.'

A sticky wicket again, but I told her about Robber, who she'd never met, lucky girl, appearing on the scene, and Norbert and Crazy Larry, but not the guns.

'You just be careful,' she said when I'd finished. 'I don't want you hurt.'

'Thanks,' I said.

'And I'm hungry now.' So we went to the restaurant.

It was cool and quiet inside and we got placed where we could see Canary Wharf and ordered a bottle of white wine.

'Not Chardonnay,' said Diane to the waiter. 'That's Liebfraumilch for the nineties.'

She was right, but then Liebfraumilch had been one of Dawn's weaknesses, although I could never understand it. I'd been thinking about Dawn a lot over the past few days. Too much.

The waiter brought a bottle of white Burgundy and wouldn't leave until Diane had expressed her approval. When we'd drunk half a glass each he came back and we ordered.

We chose chicken satay to start, and decided to share king prawns in a hot chilli sauce, soft noodles, sliced beef in red wine and mixed vegetables.

When the waiter left we lit cigarettes and Diane said, 'I don't know why you put up with me.'

'You make me forget.'

'Forget what?'

'Everything. When I'm with you I can be twenty-five with no worries. What the fuck you think when you look at me I don't know, though.'

'I see a handsome, sexy man.'

'Christ, Diane. Lucky I don't wear a hat or else I'd never get it back on.'

'You love it.'

''Course I do. Who wouldn't? But really. Why don't you find a young geezer and go and make babies?'

'I don't want babies. I don't even have a cat, you know that. Or want one of those either. Too much responsibility. I'm not going to turn into an old drudge changing nappies.'

'You'll be lonely in your old age.'

'Let me worry about that.'

'Diane,' I said. 'I used to say exactly the same. Everyone does when they look in the mirror and see a youthful reflection. But everything changes when you start getting old. You can argue with the tax man, but you either get old or die. You can't odds it.'

'You're in a morbid mood.'

'Another summer goes by and it catches up with me all of a sudden. Sorry.'

'Don't be,' she said as the food was delivered to our table. 'I'm feeling a lot better. Maybe I'll stay at your place tonight.'

And she did. And I didn't mind a bit sharing the bed with her. And however hard I tried, we didn't dislodge the guns from their hiding place under the mattress.

24

Robber got round to my place at about seven that Friday evening. He came in clutching Stonehouse's Filofax that I'd given him the previous day, with a triumphant look on his face. 'This gets better and better,' he said.

'What?' I asked.

'This book. In amongst all his business contacts and golfing buddies is one very interesting name.'

'Yeah?'

'Yeah.'

He paused.

'Well, are you going to tell me?' I said.

'Ever hear of a bloke called Tony Lambretta?'

'Is this a joke?'

'No. Tony Lambretta. He's for real, believe me.'

'He sounds like a motor scooter.'

'Some of his family are. The motor scooter firm. Or used to be. Not him. His side of the clan came over here years ago. Just before the war. Apparently his grandad or someone had a falling out with Mussolini.'

'Personally?'

'So they say. Anyway, they got here without a pot to piss in and grandad set up a tailoring firm in Hackney. Quality stuff for the carriage trade in Savile Row. They did well until the war, when they got shoved over to the Isle of Man as undesirable aliens. After the war, back to Hackney and the Hoffmann press. Anyway, to cut a long story short, young Tony's dad never went into the family firm. He had other ideas. First he opened up an ice-cream firm. Got into some heavy-duty aggro with the other ice cream-geezers. They didn't like the competition. Tony's dad came out on top. Then mini-cabs in the sixties – the same. Hard man was Tony's dad. And he had some family backing by then. A few more brothers who didn't fancy spending the rest of their lives doing hand stitching on a gent's lounge suit. Built up quite an empire, they did. Specially after the Krays went down. Mopped up a lot of their leavings in the East End. Then Tony came on board. And he was even harder than Daddy. And his name is in Stonehouse's book.'

'Could be anything. Could be from the old days, or maybe Tony likes a round of golf himself.'

'Not a fucking chance. Tony wouldn't know a golf course from a hole in the ground.'

If that was meant to be funny I didn't laugh.

'I'm surprised you don't know him yourself,' said Robber.

'I don't know everybody. The East End ain't my hangout.'

'Yeah,' Robber mused. 'And they played the legit card before you came into the job. Pretended they'd cleaned up their act. The mini-cabs turned into chauffeur hire and the ice-cream vans were bounced in for the pubs and res-taurants they used to run protection on. Sweet.'

'So what do you reckon?' I asked.

'I reckon Tony and Harry were at it together. I reckon if we can tie in Crazy Larry to Tony Lambretta we've found our bullion gang.'

'Let's see what we can do, then.'

I gave Robber the loaded nine-millimetre pistol and kept the Colt for myself, stashing it away in the pocket of my leather jacket.

'How do you reckon I'm going to catch his attention?' I said. 'You know, there we are. Crazy Larry with the rest of the members of Street Shit, and there's me, all on my lonesome.'

'For Christ's sake, Sharman. What did you do before I came along?' said Robber, producing a white paper wrap from his pocket. 'Let him have a load of this.'

I opened it. Inside was a quantity of white powder stuck together loosely. I touched my finger to the pile, then put it on my tongue. Instant freeze-out. Coke. And good stuff by the taste of it.

'There's about half a gram there,' he said. 'Cost me thirty nicker, which I'm claiming back off exes. Get that to Larry and by all accounts he'll follow you anywhere. Tell him you've got more in the motor and bring him outside.'

'Simple as that?'

'You know it's the truth. Then we have a little chat, convince him of the error of his ways. Find out if Lambretta's name rings any bells, and Bob's your uncle.'

'Never had an uncle Bob,' I said. 'Come on, let's do it.'

25

The pub was next to a stretch of dual carriageway, between two roundabouts on the main road from Croydon to Purley. Perfect for burn-ups.

The building looked like it had been flung up after the war with its slab sides of concrete and flat roof. It was in the centre of a huge car park with a hot dog wagon on one side. The wagon was closed when we arrived, but I imagined it did good business at closing time. There were just a couple of cars in the car park, but lined up neatly like dominoes in front of the public bar entrance were nine or ten motor bikes which had been chopped into hogs.

Robber parked his Sierra in a far corner close to a line of trees that backed on to a sports ground. 'Off you go,' he said. 'Have fun.'

'Cheers,' I replied as I slipped the Colt into the top of my right boot and wandered over to the pub.

I went into the saloon bar first just to get the lie of the land.

There were only two drinkers in at that relatively early hour, and they were spaced as far apart as was humanly possible. I went to the bar and ordered a pint. There was a door to my right with a sign that read: TOILETS & PUBLIC BAR. From that direction came the beat of loud music and raised voices. I sipped at my drink, then took it with me towards the door.

When I opened it I found myself in a short corridor. On

the left was the ladies', on the right the gents', and straight ahead another door with BAR written on it. The sound of music and voices was louder there.

I hesitated for a moment, wondering if a slash might not be advisable before I went in, then took my courage in one hand and my pint in the other and pushed open the door of the public bar.

Every head inside turned as I entered, and all conversation stopped. But the jukebox kept hammering out an old heavy-metal tune that I remembered from years before. Whitesnake or Deep Purple, or someone like that.

I walked to the bar and took a beaten-up stool at the end by the wall. I felt safer with something solid at my back. I sat round so that I could keep half an eye on the score or so of punters in there, and one by one they resumed their conversations and looked away from me.

They were a motley crowd of bikers, their women and hangers-on. The men were stringy-haired and dirty, wearing denim and leather with a lot of silver chains and turquoise bracelets. The women wore cut-off jeans or really short skirts. The stockings of choice were fishnet, and nearly all of them, both men and women, wore heavy motor-cycle boots. I spotted Crazy Larry right away. He was sitting at a table with a dark-haired mystery who obviously held Cher as her personal fashion icon. He held a pint in a prosthetic hand that was covered in chipped scarlet paint that probably matched the colour of his eyes, which I couldn't see for the Elvis in the seventies chrome-sided shades he wore. He stood up and went over to the jukebox and I wondered why he couldn't've been the shape and size of Norbert Green. Instead he was about six two with shithouse shoulders, and a big, almost bald head, with what remained of his hair slicked back on top. He was either growing a beard or just hadn't shaved for a week, and all in all he looked as tough as last week's sirloin left out to dry in the sun.

He fed some change into the machine and rejoined the woman. I clocked him as he walked towards her and sat down, and even through the sunglasses I saw that he noticed.

I kept looking, and after a moment he got up and ambled over to me. 'What you looking at?' he demanded.

On his good forearm I noticed that he had a tattoo that said: 'Born To Die' in Gothic script. I reckon we all are, but very few of us have to have it written prominently on our bodies to remind us.

'Larry?' I said. The tune on the jukebox had changed to some other heavy metal heroes and I had to shout over the racket.

'Who wants to know?'

'I'm a mate of Norbert Green's.' Fuck the little weasel if he thought I wasn't going to use his name.

Larry looked at me and smashed the metal hand on the bar so that my pint jumped. No one else seemed to notice, or maybe that was usual behaviour for him. 'What about him?' he demanded.

'He said you might be interested in some gear.'

'What gear?'

I took the wrap out of my pocket and handed it to him. I figured discretion was unnecessary in the back bar of the Deliverance.

He opened it and did the same finger trick as I had, wedging the wrap between two of his tin fingers and using his good hand for quality control. He looked at me and pulled what I took to be a satisfied face before sticking his nose into the paper and snarfing up most of the coke with one giant sniff. He threw his head back and knocked powder from his top lip with the back of his hand, stood for a moment, then grinned a massive, shit-eating grin. 'Good kit,' he said. 'How much you got?'

'As much as you want.'

'How much?'

'Sixty a gram. A discount on ten grams or more.'

He gripped my bicep with the red hand. 'You ain't old Bill by any chance, are you?'

'Piss off,' I said. 'That's entrapment; I'd be wasting my time. Anyway, if I was Old Bill and wanted you, I'd come in mob-handed. I'd think of something to charge you with later.'

Crazy Larry laughed. 'Yeah, I suppose you would. All right, mate, you got yourself a deal. Give.'

'No, mate,' I said, pulling my arm away from his grip. 'Not here. Outside. And just you . . . And, Larry . . .'

'Yeah?'

'COD. OK?'

26

As we walked out of the bar I saw Larry give one of his shady-looking mates a high sign. Bollocks, I thought. This is going to be trouble.

We went into the car park, past the bikes and over to the Sierra. The air stank of petrol from exhausts on the main road outside.

We got to the car and there was no sign of Robber. 'Well,' demanded Larry.

'In the hatchback,' I said, and suddenly flashed that I didn't have any keys to the car. It would've been almost bloody funny if I hadn't just realized that maybe that slash would've been a good idea after all.

'Go on, then,' he said.

Where's Robber? I kept thinking. Where's Robber? Where's bloody Robber?

Then to put the tin lid on the whole deal, Crazy Larry reaches inside the leather jacket decorated with a sheep's skull on the back with his good hand, and pulls out a dirty great buck knife with about a twelve-inch blade that gleamed brightly in the reflection of the pub lights.

'I said do it,' said Larry. 'You ponce. You ain't charging me nothin' for nothin'.'

And still no sign of sodding Robber.

Here goes, I thought, and pushed down on the hatchback button, praying that the good widow had left it unlocked.

And she had.

And as the lid slowly lifted on its hydraulic pistons there was a scream that doubly convinced me that I should've emptied my bladder when I'd had the chance, and something shot out of the boot, landed on Crazy Larry's face, knocking his Elvis shades to the ground, dug its claws into his throat and scalp, and ripped skin like tissue paper.

Larry screamed and dropped the knife, and the cat flew off Larry and headed for the trees and some sanity.

Larry put his hands to his face and wiped blood out of his eyes as Robber walked out from the shadows holding the gun in his right hand, and a cigarette in his mouth. 'Stay where you are, Larry,' he said.

I looked round, spotted the knife and picked it up. 'Where the fuck have you been?' I said.

'Watching.'

'Fucking great,' I said. 'This fucker had a sodding knife in me, and you're watching.'

'You've got a gun, ain't you?' said Robber. 'Anyhow, I've got faith in your abilities.'

Larry was looking from the gun to Robber's face and back, and blood was dripping from his chin on to his T-shirt. 'Who the fuck are you?' he said to Robber. He wasn't quite so tough now.

'Your worst nightmare,' replied Robber. 'An ex-copper with a shooter who's prepared to use it on scum like you. Now get in the car.'

As he spoke the door to the public bar burst open and the rest of the gang bundled through. Larry smiled through the blood.

'Inside,' said Robber, the cigarette bobbing up and down in his mouth.

I took out my Colt from my boot and stuck it in Larry's

side, pulling back the hammer as I did it. 'Do it, son,' I said.

'OK,' he said. 'OK. They'll catch you in a second in this heap.'

Some of the gang were only a hundred yards or so away from us when I shoved Larry into the back and piled in after him. 'Come on,' I said to Robber.

'OK,' he said and spat out the cigarette. A tiny flame glowed where the dog end lay on the tarmac, then spread and rushed across the surface of the car park and over the bikes all neatly parked in a row and then began to take hold.

'Fuck,' I said as Robber calmly got into the car and started the engine. The bikes were really going by then, and all our pursuers had turned back to try and save the machines.

'You bastard,' said Larry, and made to dive over the front seat on to Robber's back.

I clubbed him round the nose with my pistol. 'Sorry, Larry,' I said. 'But you *were* going to knife me.'

27

There was a petrol can in the passenger well of the motor, next to Robber. So it hadn't been exhaust I'd smelt when we came out of the boozer. 'Good trick,' I said. 'With the petrol. I've used that.'

'Piece of piss.'

'Tiddles done a runner, by the way,' I said.

'Never mind. It weren't her cat.'

'No wonder this thing stinks so bad,' I said. 'Did you know it was living in the back?'

'Didn't have a clue. Saved your skin, though, didn't it?'

'Which was *your* job,' I said.

'I was fixing the bikes. You can't have everything.'

'Where are we going?' said Larry suddenly. Blood from his nose was joining the blood from his face dripping down his front, and when he spoke, in the light from an approaching car's headlights I saw a big bubble of blood form on his lips, then burst.

'Somewhere quiet,' said Robber. 'This'll do.'

He'd headed away from Croydon and taken a B-road off the first roundabout, and suddenly we were in one of those bits of countryside that you can still find in the very outer ring of suburbia.

On our left was a quiet turning and Robber spun the car into it, ran up about a quarter of a mile until we came to a turnaround with no houses visible, pulled on to the verge and stopped.

He switched off the engine and wound down his window. The night was very quiet outside.

He turned round in the front seat with the Browning in his hand and switched on the courtesy light in the roof. It was yellow and dim, and occasionally fluttered as if there was a loose connection, but at least we could see Larry's blood-encrusted boat. 'OK, Larry,' Robber said. 'I've got some questions for you.'

'Like what?'

'Like who paid you to dump a body a few months ago.'

'What body?'

'The body of a mate of ours. Geezer called Harry Stonehouse. He turned up in a load of garbage bags all over the shop.'

'Bollocks,' said Larry.

'Larry, Larry, Larry,' said Robber. 'Don't be like that. Don't be a cunt all your life. Take a day off. All I want to know is who paid you. I ain't going to shop you to the coppers. This is personal.'

And involves twenty million smackers I thought, but said nothing.

'I don't know nothing,' said Larry.

'Was it a bloke called Lambretta? Tony Lambretta.'

'Never heard of him.'

'I'm getting tired of this,' said Robber. 'And I'm wasting valuable drinking time.' Then to me: 'Give us your gun, son.'

I passed over the Colt and Robber gave me the Browning. 'Keep an eye on him,' he said.

'Yes, Massah,' I said, but I did as I was told as Robber popped out the cylinder of the revolver ejecting all six rounds on to the seat next to him, then put one bullet back, closed the gun, half cocked it and spun the cylinder. 'Ever played Russian roulette?' he said to Larry, then fully cocked the little gun and stuck the muzzle into the centre of the biker's forehead.

'Fuck's sake,' said Larry, and Robber pulled the trigger.

Larry and I both jumped as the hammer went down on an empty chamber.

'Lucky boy,' said Robber, half cocked the gun again, spun the cylinder once more, pulled the hammer back all the way and put the gun back on to Larry's skull. 'Want another go?'

Larry pissed his pants at that point and the smell of human urine joined that of cat's inside the motor. I almost gagged.

'If you're lucky this time I'll add another bullet, and keep adding them till the gun's full and you're bound to lose.'

'No,' said Larry. 'I'll tell you.'

'Good boy,' said Robber. 'Come on, then.'

'It was a geezer from the other side,' Larry said. 'North London. Not Lambretta. At least I don't think so. He was a funny little fucker. Looked like one of the Marx Brothers.'

'Groucho,' I said.

'That's right,' stammered Larry.

'We've met,' I said. 'Name?'

'Jules. That's all.'

'How do you get in touch?'

'We don't.'

'How *did* you get in touch, then?'

'A garage in Dalston.'

'Whereabouts?'

Larry hesitated and Robber pushed the Colt harder against his forehead and said, 'You want me to pull this trigger?'

Larry told us. He was very exact. By the time he'd

finished I almost knew how much they charged to service a car.

'All right, Larry, we believe you,' said Robber. 'You can go now.'

Larry gathered the tattered remains of his dignity around him and fumbled for the door handle.

'Just one thing before you go,' said Robber.

'What?'

'That hand. Does it come off?'

''Course.'

'Go on, then.'

'What?'

'Get it off.'

'Why?'

'I want it.'

'No.'

'My mate's got a fully loaded automatic stuck in your side, Larry. Now one thing's for certain, if *he* plays Russian roulette with that you're going to lose first time. So don't fuck about. Get the hand off and then piss off. Mind you, you've already done that, ain't you?' And he grinned evilly.

'Bastards,' said Larry as he started fumbling with the fastening of the prosthetic. 'I'll get you for this.'

'Sure,' said Robber. 'Just get on with it and me and my mate can get down the boozer.'

28

I pushed Crazy Larry out of the car as Robber started the engine, swung the motor in a tight U-turn and we sped back the way we'd come. I clambered into the passenger seat carrying the scarlet prosthetic hand in mine, dropped it next to the empty petrol can and lit a cigarette for each of us. 'What shall I do with that?' I said.

'Chuck it out or keep it as a souvenir,' said Robber.

'Souvenir, I think,' I said. 'You never know when you might need a hand.'

'Very amusing,' said Robber dryly.

'You took a chance with that bullet, didn't you?' I said. 'I never thought you'd pull the trigger.'

'Spin the cylinder of a revolver with one bullet in it, and generally gravity pulls it down to the bottom. Not always, but mostly. It was a calculated risk.'

'A calculated risk for him, but not for you. Would you have kept on putting bullets in?'

'Sure. I had to make the cunt talk, didn't I?'

'Sometimes you scare me, Robber,' I said.

'Me too.'

We headed towards London, and on the other side of Croydon Robber said, 'Let's have that drink.'

He pulled into the car park of another pub and stopped the motor. When he got out he looked round and when he was satisfied there was no one about he went to the front and back of the car and removed a set of number plates that he'd taped over the genuine ones. 'Just in case our boy has a good memory and some way of finding out where the motor's registered,' he explained. 'I wouldn't want anyone popping round to see the widow woman when I'm not there.'

'You think of everything.'

'I try.'

We went into the boozer which was mid-evening busy and Robber went straight to the bar and ordered large scotches for both of us, and paid. Playing around with the pistol must've been more traumatic than I'd thought. We took our drinks to a corner table. 'Result time,' said Robber after he'd downed half his whisky.

'Jules from Dalston,' I said. 'Know him?'

'Not yet. But you do.'

'Yeah. And I'd love to see him again.'

'You will.'

'What next, then?'

'They know both of us, that much is certain from the other night when Jules and his mates visited you. So we can't just turn up and ask them for a quick MOT. We're going to have to have a shufti round on the QT. We need another car. We can't use either of ours. Any ideas?'

'I can get a motor or two. No bother. A phone call'll do it. First thing.'

'Good. Tomorrow's Saturday. So get a car and we'll take a trip up Dalston way. They might not even be open. But it'll be worth it just to have a look-see. I still reckon Lambretta's at the back of all this. The area fits if nothing else. Then if we come up with nothing within a few days I reckon we'll have to go inside one dark night and see what we can find. You up for that?'

'Lovely,' I said. 'A bit of B&E. It's every boy's dream.'

He winked at me and said, 'Your round, I think.'

29

After a few more drinks Robber dropped me back at home. I left him the 9mm and took the now fully-loaded Colt with me. I kept it in one hand as I went up the stairs. If there were any more late-night uninvited callers, at least I wanted to be on equal terms with them.

But when I got up to my flat it was empty and undisturbed, and I stuck the revolver back into my waistband as I put the kettle on for tea.

I'd also bought Crazy Larry's prosthetic hand with me. I had just the place for it. By the window I kept this monster cheese plant that was threatening to take over the whole flat. I stuck the hand in the earth, fingers up, so it looked as if someone was trying to dig themselves out of the pot. I wondered what Judith would make of it, but the weird way her brain's beginning to work, I reckoned she'd think it was cool. Our minds work similarly, and I feel a bit sorry for her on that front. But at least we laugh at the same things.

I went to bed with the gun under my pillow.

The next morning I called up Charlie, my mate who works in the motor trade, early. 'Hello, Charles,' I said breezily.

'Don't tell me. You want to borrow a car and not pay for it.'

'And a very good morning to you, Charles. How is every little thing?'

'Every little thing is fine. It's the big things like you that's the problem. What kind of car do you want?'

'Something discreet.'

'With bullet-proof glass, no doubt.'

'I think I'll pass on that particular optional extra. Just an ordinary car will do.'

'What about that heap of yours?'

'No good, mate. This is just for a bit of surveillance and mine's cover's blown.'

'More nutters with guns, I suppose.'

'Just a little watching brief.'

'All right. I'll take your word for it. As it goes I took a late-model Audi on the bounce last week. You can have that. How long for?'

'Couple of days.'

'Usual deal. You sort out the insurance and pay for any damage.'

'No probs.'

'It's here when you're ready.'

'Cheers, mate. You're a friend.'

'So are you. But do you always have to be a friend in need?'

'Very amusing. Listen I'll be up in a few.'

'I'll be here.'

After I'd talked to Charlie I called up Robber on his mobile. 'I've got a motor,' I said. 'What time shall I pick you up?'

'It's nine-thirty now. In about an hour. People like Jules don't generally like to be out until the streets are aired. Specially on a Saturday.'

''K. I'll see you then.' And I rang off.

I made myself a desultory breakfast and at ten I took my BMW up to Charlie's used car lot. There was a shiny black

Audi waiting on the forecourt. Charlie was leaning on it talking to one of his mechanics. 'Hello, Nick,' he said. 'Here it is, mate.'

'Looks nice, Charlie,' I said.

'Keep it that way, willya. I've got quite a few grand tied up in this little item.'

'Trust me.'

'I have before, and look where it's got me.'

I got behind the wheel and the car started on the button. 'Sounds good,' I said.

'Got time for tea?'

'Sure.'

'Organize a couple of teas, Tom,' said Charlie to the mechanic.

I chatted to Charlie about not much until the tea arrived, and we drank it together, and I smoked one of his Benson's. Then around ten twenty-five I gave the keys to my car to Charlie and took the short run to Robber's lodgings in the Audi. The car was fully loaded and ran smoothly, and if it hadn't been for the uncomfortable lump the Colt made stuck in the back waistband of my jeans, I might've thought I was on a pleasure trip.

30

We drove over the river, and following Crazy Larry's instructions we found the garage easily. 'He didn't lie,' said Robber. 'At least the place exists.'

'It's the power of Mr Colt,' I said, and Robber grinned.

The garage was small and scruffy, and on the corner of a main road and a cul-de-sac. There were three cars parked outside, including a bright red N-reg Ferrari. The only sign of humanity was a greasy-looking mechanic in dirty overalls working under the bonnet of a Vauxhall Cavalier. I parked the Audi opposite, on the corner of another side road two turnings down, so that we could see the garage, but we weren't obvious. Robber had brought along a pair of binoculars, and the widow had made up a big pack of sandwiches and filled a jumbo thermos with hot, sweet coffee.

It was just like a picnic.

Nothing occurred all morning, and Robber and I listened to the radio, nattered about not much, and ate and drank and smoked. At lunchtime Groucho, or Jules, or whatever his name was, came strolling down the main drag and went into the garage. He was still wearing his long overcoat. He had a few words with the mechanic who rolled the Cavalier under cover and they locked up. The mechanic got into one of the cars on the small forecourt and Groucho took off his nanny, chucked it into the back of the Ferrari, got in and drove off too.

'Nice wheels,' said Robber. 'Let's follow him.'

When the Ferrari pulled on to the street I fell in two cars behind, and although the Italian motor was very low-slung it wasn't difficult to follow its progress because of its bright colour and the fact that Groucho was a slow and careful driver.

He headed west and ended up outside a block of flats in Hampstead – the nice part of Hampstead – retrieved his coat and went inside.

'That's either his place, a mate's or his bird's,' said Robber. 'But at least we've got somewhere. We can hang around here all day on the off-chance, or split.'

'I don't mind,' I said.

'I think it's enough for today. Let's call it off until Monday. At least we know Larry was telling us some of the truth. And we know where to find Groucho if we want him. We'll watch the garage again Monday morning, see if any more of your mates turn up.'

'Good enough,' I said. 'What you doing tomorrow?'

'Taking the widow to the pictures and out for a ruby.'

'Watch yourself,' I said.

'Sure. What about you?'

'I think I'll see if *my* widow's about. I should report in.'

'What are you going to tell her?'

'Not much.'

31

As soon as I got back home I called Nancy Stonehouse. 'I think we should get together,' I said.

'Sounds good to me.'

'To talk about the case.'

'What else?'

'What are you doing tomorrow?'

'Not much. Come over for lunch.'

'Sounds good. What time?'

'One suit you?'

'Terrific.'

'See you then.' And we made our farewells and hung up.

I was on her doorstep at the prescribed hour, a bottle of decent red and another of white in a Thresher's bag. I was wearing a new pair of Levi's, a checked flannel shirt, my disreputable leather jacket and the official boots from the Grand Ole Opry that I'd bought from a shop in Covent Garden. I looked the business and I knew it.

She was wearing jeans too. A thin and faded old pair that showed her backside off to its best advantage, and a T-shirt sans bra that did the same to her tits.

'Hello, Nancy,' I said.

'Hello, Nick,' she said, and I realized that after all this time we were finally friends.

I grinned and offered her the bottles. 'Something towards lunch.'

'Best offer I've had all day.'

She showed me into the living room and poured out huge gin and tonics for us both. 'Sit down,' she said.

I took the armchair and she sat on the sofa opposite. 'Anything happening?' she asked.

I took out my cigarettes and offered her one. She refused but said, 'You go ahead. There's an ashtray behind you. So,' she said when I'd lit up.

'We've made some progress.'

'We?'

'I've taken on a partner for the case.'

What I didn't tell her was that he'd done most of the work. It was me that felt like the partner. And a junior partner at that.

'Anyone I know?' she asked.

'You might. He's an ex-copper. DI Robber as was.'

'Sure I know him. Dirty teeth and shirt.'

'He's cleaned up his act. Or at least his sister cleaned it up for him. He retired and went to stay with her. She banged the drum and he did the dance.'

'Good for her. So what progress?'

'Early days yet, Nancy. But we're getting somewhere. Give us a little longer and I might have something more concrete for you.'

'Can't you tell me now?'

'It's not come together properly yet. Trust me. Soon.'

'So why did you want to see me?'

'Because I like you, as a matter of fact. And there was no one else I'd rather see. And it was Sunday, and I was all alone. You don't mind, do you?'

She smiled. 'Not at all, Nick. I get lonely here by myself too.'

'Tell me about it.'

'But I bet you're not by yourself much.'

116

I thought of Diane. 'Not all the time. But enough for it to get to me. I just fancied seeing you. And you're a good cook.'

'Always the same Nick.'

'I try. What is for lunch by the way?'

'Roast beef and Yorkshire.'

'Sounds all right to me.'

'And if you're lucky there might even be some afters.'

We gave the gin bottle more of a caning, and Nancy kept vanishing into the kitchen and bringing back the most delicious culinary smells when she returned. Finally, at about two-fifteen she came back for the last time and said, 'Luncheon is served.'

And it was well worth the wait. The woman could cook up a storm. The meat was pink and tender, the potatoes were crisp on the outside and like mush beneath. The half-dozen or so vegetables she'd baked or boiled were just perfect. And the peach pie. I won't bore you with the details, but I had three slices.

'That was the business,' I said when every plate was clean.

'There's plenty more,' she said. 'I still always buy for two.'

'Couldn't manage a thing,' I said. 'Except perhaps some of your coffee and brandy.'

'It's ready in the living room,' she said.

'You're a marvel.'

We left the dishes and went back to where we'd started. The room was very quiet and I could feel the tension mounting. 'Is there any football on TV?' I asked.

She gave me a really dirty look and I just grinned, and suddenly she caught on and started to laugh. We both laughed then, but hers took on an edge of hysteria and I thought she was going to throw a wobbly, before tears came and her body was racked with sobs.

I went over and held her. 'It's all right,' I said. 'It'll soon be over.'

She clung on to me, and for a minute I thought she was playing the oldest trick in the book, but there were no kissings or strokings. She just clung on for dear life until the sobs began to subside.

Then she pulled away. 'Sorry, Nick,' she said. 'I don't know what came over me.'

'I do.' It happens to me all the time. 'You've just had enough.'

'You can say that again.' She moved up to the other end of the sofa. 'I must look a mess.'

Just the opposite. She looked great. Streaky mascara and puffed-up eyes and all.

'No,' I said. 'You look fine.'

She went off and washed her face and repaired her make-up. When she came back, we just sat there for the rest of the afternoon. Me back in the armchair, her on the sofa. We talked about old times, and Harry, and more old times, and after a bit what we'd been to each other. Precious little I'm afraid at the time. We were much better friends now.

Slowly the room darkened and she asked, 'Are you hungry?'

'After that lunch? No thanks.'

'Do you have to go home?'

'Not now. Not tonight. Tomorrow I've got some work on the case.'

'So don't go.'

'I won't.'

And I didn't.

32

I picked up Robber the next morning the same time as I had on Saturday. We drove back to the garage and parked in the same spot as previously. Only this time I had to keep an eye out for traffic wardens.

The same Ferrari was there, and the same mechanic, only this time he was crawling under a Jag. Once again there was no sign of Groucho. 'Do you think he's got an office?' I said.

'Something like that. Doesn't want to get his hands dirty here.'

A second mechanic drove up shortly after in a white Escort van and joined his mate on the Jaguar. We sat and waited for something more interesting to happen.

'How was the widow?' asked Robber after a few minutes.

I knew he was going to ask that sooner or later. 'Fine,' I replied.

'Have a good day?'

'Yeah. She made me lunch.'

'Coo.'

'How about *your* widow?'

'Fine.'

'Have a good day?'

'Yeah. I treated her to Harrison Ford and a lamb Masala.'

'Coo,' I said.

And that was Monday. At six Groucho showed, closed up the place and went back to Hampstead.

'One more day,' said Robber. 'And we'll have to get there early. Find out where Groucho hangs out.'

The next morning we were there at eight. Groucho showed at nine and Robber followed him. We figured that although Groucho knew him, he wouldn't expect to see him in Dalston. It was all we could do, and we had to take a chance. He called me on my mobile ten minutes later to tell me that Groucho had gone to ground in an office over a betting shop, half a mile or so away. 'This is the place we've got to watch,' he said, and I drove up to where he was waiting and we parked in a supermarket car park so that we could easily see the front door of Groucho's building.

'I had a look round the back,' said Robber. 'There's a fire escape, but the yard there is full of crap and doesn't look like anyone's been through it for years. Any comings and goings are round the front. At least I hope they are.'

They were. Both the young Asian and the bloke built like a steamroller called by before the morning was much older. Plus another three or four equally dodgy-looking characters.

'Wouldn't mind being a fly on the wall in there,' remarked Robber as yet another villainous individual sidled in through the door.

Men, and it was only men, came and went all day, but no one except the trio that had called on me did we know.

At six Groucho came out and walked in the direction of the garage. 'Shit,' said Robber. 'Want another trip to Hampstead?'

'But he might not be going to Hampstead,' I said.

And he wasn't.

This time he headed east and didn't stop until he was on

the outskirts of Romford. The nice outskirts of Romford where the houses were all seriously detached and in their own grounds, mostly behind high walls, and where uniformed security men patrolled in little blue vans. We dropped back until Groucho stopped outside an imposing set of iron gates, said something into an entryphone and was admitted.

'The Laurels,' said Robber, noting the name on the wall next to the gate as we went past. 'I'll check that out.'

We went home then. It seemed pointless to wait. There's nothing more boring than surveillance.

We agreed to meet early the next morning, and once again I called for Robber. On the way to Dalston his mobile rang, and when he broke the connection after listening for less than a minute, with only grunts as his contribution to the conversation, he hung up and beamed at me.

'Bingo,' he said. 'Got the fucker. The Laurels is owned by a certain Mrs Tony Lambretta.'

'Mrs?'

'Oldest one in the book. Anything happens to Tony financially, or he gets his collar felt and the court confiscates. He owns nothing. All in the little woman's name.'

'Till the little woman runs off with the gardener.'

'Not this little woman. Tony'd flay the skin off her alive if she as much as looked cross-eyed at the gardener. And she knows it.'

'So. More results.'

'No more results than my ex-employers could've got with a little digging.'

'Perhaps we were just lucky. Or good.'

'We're good, Nick, but not so good that the Bill couldn't've followed this up. Specially with their resources. No, mate. Something very funny is going on here.'

121

That was what I was afraid of.

'So what next?' I asked.

'Next we go and have a look round Groucho's office. We'll do it tonight after he's safely tucked up.'

33

We watched the office all that day too, and nothing much occurred apart from the faces we were coming to know popping in and out. Groucho did his usual routine come six o'clock, and this time he went back to Hampstead. When he was settled we drove back to Dalston and found a pub that did food. We stayed there until closing, and then I drove around in the car until after midnight.

The supermarket car park was empty and I tucked the Audi away in the far corner in the shadow of the back of the building. Then Robber and I crossed the main road and went down a side street to the alley at the back of the betting shop. He'd been right about the crap in the back yard. We climbed over the fence, picked our way through piles of wet newspapers and black sacks that rustled ominously as if full of a plague of rats, to the fire escape. We climbed the metal steps to the first floor and Robber checked the door and windows. 'All tight,' he whispered. 'But I've got just the thing.' From under his jacket he pulled out a short crowbar.

'Subtle,' I said.

'Don't worry about it. They ain't gonna report this to the coppers,' he said. 'I bet they'd just love a visit from CID.'

He inserted the sharp end of the bar into the crack between door and jamb and leant on it. With a terrible sound of splitting wood and rasping metal the door opened.

To me it sounded as loud as a seven-car pile-up, but no one in the vicinity seemed to notice. Maybe that sort of noise was par for the course at midnight in Dalston.

'Come on, then,' said Robber, and we went inside.

We'd both brought small torches from the car, and in their light we started to take a look round the place. It was just two rooms, both containing desks, chairs and filing cabinets. Off one of the rooms was a toilet, off the other a tiny kitchen. We went through the place and found absolutely nothing. The filing cabinets contained a few old newspapers, the desk drawers were full of air, there was no fax or answering machine, and the milk in the kitchen was off. A big zero.

'So what the fuck do they do here all day?' I asked when our fruitless search was done.

'Fuck knows,' said Robber. 'Plan bullion blags, I suppose. Come on, let's get out of here. We're wasting our time.'

We left the way we'd come and climbed over the fence back into the alley.

As we walked towards its junction with the side street someone stepped out from behind a skip that almost blocked the alley and said, 'Find what you were looking for?'

34

It was sodding Groucho, overcoat on, and a mean-looking silenced automatic snug in his german. 'Not much to see inside, is there?' he said.

Robber and I turned as one to do a runner, and behind us stood the young Asian and Steamroller, also armed with silenced weapons. 'Shit,' I said.

'Shit, is right,' said the Asian. 'You two really are inept.'

'Is that right?' said Robber.

'Didn't you think that thick biker would tell?' said the Asian. 'And fancy nicking his hand. That was hardly cricket.'

Cricket, I thought. Who did this fucker think he was? Imran Khan?

'Never mind about that,' said Groucho to the Asian. Then to us: 'Did you think we wouldn't suss? We've been watching you all week.'

And I never noticed, I thought.

'And we've been watching you,' said Robber. 'Did you have a pleasant evening with Tony Lambretta?'

'Don't think you're so clever,' said Groucho. 'You only know as much as we want you to know. And sod all use it'll be to you.'

'So what are you going to do?' said Robber. 'Shoot us?'

'Yeah,' said Groucho and fired his gun. It made no more sound than someone spitting on the pavement, and the round hit Robber in the chest. In the faint light from the street lamps in the side road I saw a look of surprise spread over his face and he put his hand on his front where the bullet had entered.

Things went mental for about ten seconds then, although thinking back it seemed like two hours and everyone moved in slow motion like a Sam Peckinpah movie.

Robber turned to me, the look of surprise turning to horror. I reached for the Colt that was in the waistband of my jeans and I backed against the fence behind me as the Asian and Steamroller fired simultaneously. The Asian's bullet hit Robber in the side and Steamroller's hit the fence beside me, knocking a huge splinter out of the wood. I found my Colt and dragged it out, cocking the hammer as I did it, but it snagged in the material, and before I could fire, Groucho turned his gun in my direction. I saw his finger tighten on the trigger and the stab of flame as he fired, and I can almost swear I saw the red hot bullet leave the muzzle heading for me just as Robber staggered into me. He took Groucho's bullet in the shoulder, and the slug passed clear through him, showering me with blood, and the bullet spun up and hit me in the head like I'd been clouted with a piece of lead pipe. We both went down and I must've passed out for a few seconds. When I came to I was underneath Robber and could feel blood pumping out of his chest wound and soaking me. The alley was empty and I was bleeding like a stuck pig myself from the wound in my head which throbbed like the worst hangover head-ache I'd ever had. My eyes were full of blood and I reached up and wiped the thick, warm goo away to clear them. I had no idea how long I'd been out, but looking at the state of Robber I knew it had been too long. He was dying in front of my eyes from his wounds and loss of blood.

I rolled him gently off me, stuck the gun I was still

holding into my pocket and felt the bulk of the portable phone I'd been carrying around since he'd given it to me. Thank God, I thought, dragged it out, prayed that it hadn't been broken, flicked it on, saw the display light up, dialled nine-nine-nine, and pushed the 'SEND' button.

'Emergency. Which service do you require?' a female voice said into my ear.

'Ambulance. Quickly. There's a man dying here.'

'What's happened?'

'He's been shot at least three times and he's losing blood fast.'

'Can you give me your name and location? As you're calling from a mobile station we cannot find you from the number we have.'

Shit, they had the mobile number. Modern technology is hell on people's privacy.

'At the back of a row of shops off Dalston High Street,' I said. 'Opposite the Gateway supermarket. We're in an alley behind a betting shop. I don't know the name of the side road. Look, he's dying. For God's sake get an ambulance here quickly.'

'It's on its way. And the police.'

'Whatever. Just hurry them up, there's not much time.' And I cut off the call before she could ask who I was again, and I wondered in who's name Robber had put the telephones he'd bought.

Robber's chest wound was sucking badly and blood was still pumping out, and I cradled his inert body with one arm and stuck the other hand over the bullet wound and pressed down hard to try to quell the flow.

He opened his eyes then, looked straight into mine in the thin light and said, 'Don't let me die.'

'You ain't going to fucking die,' I replied, and he stopped breathing. Just like that.

No, I thought. Not you too. Not another. Not another person close to me dying. I won't let this happen. Not again. 'Jack,' I yelled. 'Jack, you fucker. Don't do this to me. Don't you fucking dare, you bastard.' And I took my hand away from his wound and struck him in the face as hard as I could. And miraculously, he gulped deep in his throat and started breathing again just as I heard the sound of sirens in the distance.

35

Robber was still breathing, though with difficulty, when the ambulance and police car arrived simultaneously.

The paramedics took over, fixing up a drip and field dressings and informing the hospital that an emergency gunshot wound case would be coming in within minutes. I stood with my back against the fence, my legs trembling, covered in Robber's and my own blood that had started dripping down my face again, and one of the coppers from the squad car said to me, 'Exactly what happened here?'

'Dunno,' I replied. 'I was walking home when I heard someone shout and I found him.'

The copper looked at me cross-eyed and shone his torch on to my face. 'You've been hurt yourself.'

'I banged my head on the edge of the skip,' I said, gesturing in its direction. 'When I found him.'

'What's your name?' the second copper asked.

'Harvey. John Harvey.' He's a writer. I had one of his books on my bedside table at home, and it was the best I could come up with at short notice.

'Address?'

I hesitated. I didn't have a clue about any local street names.

'Twenty-two . . .' I hesitated again.

The first copper looked at the second, and I saw the faint nod he gave his colleague. 'I think we'd better have the medics look at you then take you to hospital. You're bleeding badly,' he said. 'Then maybe you'll remember where you live.'

'It's all right,' I protested. 'Just a scratch.'

'No, sir,' said the first copper, still a little unsure. And it was the little I was living in, and he took hold of my left arm.

'Look out, he's got a gun,' yelled the other policeman, and I had. As the first one got hold of me, I'd slipped my right hand into my jacket pocket and brought out the Colt and stuck it into his face.

'Back off, boys,' I said. 'And give me some air.'

The paramedics looked up from their work. 'Don't stop,' I shouted. 'Keep going. I'm not going to hurt you.'

They did as they were told, as I forced the two old Bill out of the alley and into the side street. 'Start walking,' I ordered. 'In that direction.' And pointed away from the main road. 'And don't look back.'

They did as they were told, and I walked up to the squad car, shot out the front tyre and legged it towards the car park where I'd left the Audi, my head feeling like it was going to drop off at any moment.

36

I got into the car and leant my aching head against the window, leaving a smear of blood on the glass. I started it up and swung out of the car park and headed towards central London. There was no one in sight. As I drove off, the ambulance pulled out of the side turning and raced off with its siren wailing. There was no sign of the two coppers.

I drove slowly, wiping more blood out of my eyes and wondering where the hell to go. Between the police and Groucho's boys I couldn't go home. I thought about trying Nancy Stonehouse. But if the police identified Robber and tied him to me and the case, the filth would be all over Fulham like a rash before the sun rose. And what if Jack died? It would be down to me. Another fuck-up in a career so full of them I should get mentioned in dispatches. Fuck me, I was certainly going to get mentioned in the Met's daily orders. Pulling an unlicensed gun on two police officers, destroying police property, leaving the scene of a crime. Plus whatever else they could pin on me in the way of petty or serious misdemeanours. Outstanding behaviour. I was a one-man crime wave, and it was still a long time till breakfast.

As I drove sedately through the East End I saw lots of police vehicles heading in the direction I was coming from, blue lights flashing and sirens screaming, but no one took any notice of me.

So it had to be Diane, and I hated to involve her but I had no choice. She was the only friend I could turn to, even if I screwed her up in the process. I pulled out my portable phone and keyed in her number. Since I'd known her she'd left her parents' home in Essex and rented a tiny flat in Maida Vale. It was nothing to do with me, but thank Christ she had. She answered on the tenth ring, sounding sleepy and disorientated.

'Whassamatta?' she said when she realized who it was. 'Do you know what time it is?'

'Sorry, sweetheart,' I said. 'I'm in a bit of trouble. I need a place to stay for a bit.'

'What kind of trouble?' She sounded wide awake then.

'Bad trouble. I'll tell you all about it later.'

'And you want to stay here?'

'If I can. If I can't, don't worry about it.'

''Course you can.'

Relief washed over me. 'Thanks,' I said.

'Where are you?'

'Heading your way.'

'How long?'

'Twenty minutes.'

'OK.'

''Bye. And thanks again.' And I cut her off.

I left the car close to Maida Vale tube which was about five minutes' walk from Diane's flat, or more like five minutes' lurch for me, as I felt pretty weird when I got out of the Audi.

I kept to what shadows there were as I cut through the side streets to her place, which was on the ground floor of a big old semi-detached mansion close to a park.

The lights were on behind drawn curtains when I arrived. I climbed the five stone steps to her front door and leant

132

against one of the columns that supported the porch and rang the bell of her flat. She answered in a moment with a dressing-gown over her nightie and let me into the hall.

As soon as she saw me in the hall light I saw her face go white. 'Nick,' she said. 'What the hell's happened? You're covered in blood. And your head.'

'A bit of grief darlin',' I said. 'Nothing to get worried about.' And I passed out again.

I came to as she was helping me up. 'Lean on me,' she said. 'I've got to call a doctor.'

'No. No doctors.'

'Nick. You're losing so much blood.'

'It's not all mine,' I said. 'Jack Robber's been shot.'

'Your friend.'

'The very one.'

She helped me over to the sofa in her living room. 'Get something to cover it,' I said, wavering on my feet. 'I don't want any evidence that I've been here. You could be in big trouble.'

She left me standing there and ran into the bedroom and came back with a bed sheet that she threw over the sofa. Meanwhile I'd taken off my leather jacket, rolled it up inside out and dropped it on the floor. As soon as the sofa was covered I fell on to the cushions. 'Jesus,' I said, 'but I feel rough.'

She went out again and came back with a wet flannel, moved a table lamp and examined my head, dabbing at the wound to get a better view. 'That's a bad cut, Nick,' she said. 'What hit you?'

'A spent bullet, I think,' I said. 'It went through Robber's shoulder and came up and hit me. It must've been deflected off a bone.'

'God,' she said. 'But it needs stitches. You must go to hospital.'

'Fine. I'd be in jail as soon as I left. No. No hospital.'

'But it must be stitched.'

'Then you do it.'

'What?'

'You heard. You stitch it. You repaired my old jeans.'

'For Christ's sake, this is a bit different.'

'Not much. They're both old, frayed material that's seen better days.'

'Oh, Nick.'

'Have you got anything to drink?' I asked.

'Like what?'

'Hard liquor, preferably.'

'There's a bottle of scotch.'

'Get it. And any aspirin or paracetamol.'

'Sure.'

She scurried off for a third time and came back with a nearly full bottle of Whyte & Mackay and a box of fifty paracetamol. I washed down half a dozen of the painkillers with the whisky and she said, 'Take it easy with those.'

'Sod it,' I said. 'My head feels like a fucking horse has kicked it.'

'It looks like it too,' she remarked, which sort of closed that subject.

I lay back and she helped me off with the rest of my clothes apart from my boxer shorts which seemed to be the only item not covered in gore. 'Wash those, will you,' I said. 'And rinse off my jacket and boots. Sorry, darlin', but I can't manage on my own.'

'As soon as I've seen to you.'

'And Jack,' I said. 'I've got to find out how he is.' I kept nipping at the scotch as we talked.

134

'Was he hurt badly?'

'About as badly as can be. He stopped breathing for a bit.'

'Oh, Nick, I am sorry.'

'And he saved my life,' I said, my tongue getting heavy in my mouth. 'He stepped between me and a bullet.'

Then I passed out for a third time. It was getting to be a habit.

I came to as pain went searing through my head like a hot wire, and sat up sharply. 'Be still,' said Diane, needle and cotton in her hand. 'Or it'll hurt more.'

I swallowed more whisky and went under again.

When I woke up the next time I was in Diane's bed. It was daylight and I was alone. The top of my head felt like it was coming off, and I touched the wound with my fingertips. It was dry and scabby and felt as tight as a drum skin. I tried to call her, but the effort was too much, and I sank down once more into a cold blackness tinged with hot scarlet.

I could feel myself shivering with the cold, then sweating with the heat, and from somewhere a warm, naked body held me tight and rocked me into a delicious healing sleep.

Then another awakening, to the rich smell of some kind of cooked meat. I was starving and Diane was sitting on the edge of the bed with a tray on her knee. On the tray was a bowl of broth, and I can't remember when anything smelled as good.

'Christ, but I'm hungry,' I said, and sat up, sending a dart of pain through my head. But not so much pain as before, and it didn't last as long.

'Are you going to go away again?' she said. 'You keep on waking up and passing out again.'

'I don't think so. At least not until I've eaten that.' She put the tray on to my lap and I dived into the broth. It was delicious.

'Thank God. I was so worried.'

A sudden freezing fear cut through me. 'How long has it been?' I asked, my spoon half-way to my mouth.

'Three days.'

'Three days. You're joking.'

'I've never been more serious. I thought you were going to die. You had a terrible fever. You were freezing, then boiling. I got into bed with you. It was the only thing I could think to do.'

'God.' Then another thought struck me. 'Jack. How is he?'

'Serious but stable. Whatever that means. He's in Intensive Care.'

'How do you know?'

'I phoned the hospital. It's been on TV since the morning after you arrived here.'

'Who did you say you were?'

'His niece. But I could only phone once. The police came on and gave me a hard time.'

'Where did you phone from? Not here.'

'No. I used a phone box a mile away. You made me promise not to use my phone, or your mobile.'

'When?'

'When you were delirious that night and the next day. You talked a lot. I was so frightened I almost called a doctor.'

'I'm glad you didn't. What did you do?'

'What you said. I stitched the wound myself. It'll scar.'

'What's one more? Thanks, Diane. You're a genius.'

'Not really. But the wound started to go septic a bit,

even though I used white thread and boiled it, and sterilized the needle. Thank God it's cleared up.'

I passed her back the empty soup bowl and made as if to get up.

'Where are you going?'

'To the toilet, then out. I've got things to do. What about the toilet, by the way? You know, when I was out of it.'

'I rigged up a bed pan.'

'Lovely.'

'And you're not going anywhere. At least not for a few days. You need to build up your strength.'

'But there's so much I need to do.'

'It'll have to wait.'

37

And she was right. When I got up I could hardly stand, and she had to help me to the bathroom.

When I'd done the necessary I came back and almost collapsed into bed. 'Shit,' I said. 'What's happened to me?'

'Blood loss and lack of nourishment. You'll be OK.'

'I hope so.'

'I've got something to show you,' she said and went out of the room, returning a minute later with a pile of newspapers in her hands.

Robber and I had made the front page big time. At least in the *Standard*. In the daily newspapers we were relegated to the centre spread or next to the topless bimbo.

'Shit,' I said again, reading about our exploits. 'Fame at last.'

No mention was made of names, and the gist of the story was that a couple of East End villains had fallen out and decided to settle their differences with guns. One was near death in hospital, the other had threatened the police and escaped. There was no suggestion that other parties had been involved.

But a little digging would prove otherwise. Robber had the bullets from at least two separate guns inside him, and if I was the other face involved, who had wanted him dead bad enough to shoot him at least three times, why the hell had I phoned the emergency services and then stuck around waiting for them to arrive?

No. Old Bill knew more than they were releasing to the media, and I was willing to bet that at least a part of it was Robber's identity, and possibly mine too. I wondered if he'd talked, if indeed he was able to, and I had a dreadful premonition that he was dead.

'I've got to phone the hospital,' I said. 'Which one is it, by the way?'

'Don't you remember?'

'No.'

'Dalston General. You told me that too.'

And I suddenly remembered the paramedic reporting to his control over the radio.

'I forgot,' I said. 'I've got to phone them.'

'Where from?'

'I don't know. That's why I told you not to use the phone here, or my mobile. There's too many places with call ID for my liking.'

'You can't go out.'

'I know. I don't think I'd make the end of the street. But there must be a way.' I snapped my fingers. ''Course there is. The widow.'

'Who?'

'Robber's landlady. She'll know the score. Is my book in my jacket pocket?'

She nodded and went and fetched it. I looked up the number that Robber had given me, picked up my portable from the side of the bed and punched out the number. It was answered on the third ring by a woman.

'Mrs Brody?' I said.

'Yes?'

'My name's Sharman. Nick Sharman,' I said. 'It's about Jack.'

'Mr Sharman,' she replied. 'Where are you? The police are looking for you.'

'Are they there now?'

'No. But they're never far away.'

'So they know who he is.'

'They knew the morning after it happened.'

'You know I didn't shoot him, don't you?'

'Jack told me all about you. I believe you were his friend.'

'*Were.* He's not . . . ?' I felt the cold hand of fear again.

'No, no. I'm sorry, that came out wrong.'

I breathed out with relief. 'How is he?' I asked.

'It's not good. He's still in Intensive Care.'

'Have you seen him?'

'Yes.'

'Can he talk?'

'No. Nothing anyone can understand, anyway.'

'What do the doctors say?'

'They don't know.'

'Sod it . . . Sorry.'

'Don't mention it. I've heard far worse. Where are you?'

'It's better that you don't know and that no one knows I called. I've been shot too. Have you told the police what he was doing?'

'No. Jack and I are old friends. We know how to keep each other's secrets. My past hasn't been all it should be.'

I guessed she'd been a brass or on the hoist or something. That was good. The last thing I needed was an irate solid citizen bleating about everything she knew.

'At least he's still alive,' I said. 'He stopped me from being badly hurt the other night. I owe him one. Tell him if you can, if he can understand, without anyone else hearing. And tell him I'll get in to see him before long. Somehow. I'll call again soon. I'm glad he's got you.'

'He's got his sister too. She's come up and moved into his room.'

'Is she as bad as he makes out?'

'No. But she's gunning for you.'

An unfortunate choice of words, I thought.

'Then it's better no one knows I've called.'

'They won't from me.'

'Good,' I said. 'I'll be in touch.'

We said goodbye and I turned off the phone.

Then I saw two sets of keys on the bedside table next to the Detective Special.

'Christ,' I said. 'The car.'

'It's gone.'

'How do you know?'

'You told me what it was and where you'd parked it. I went and had a look for it the next afternoon but there was no sign.'

'We must've had a hell of a lot of conversations when I was out of it.'

'We did. Who's Wanda?'

'An old friend. She's dead now.'

'You talked to her a lot.'

'We had a lot of unfinished business,' I said, turned on the phone again and called Charlie's garage from memory.

He answered swiftly too.

'Charlie,' I said.

'Sharman,' he said back. Bad news when old mates call you by your surname. 'What the fuck have you been up to now?'

'The police found the car.'

'Yes they sodding well did. In Maida Vale with the upholstery covered in blood. It'll cost me a fortune to get it right.'

'That was mostly my blood,' I said. 'Thanks for the sympathy.'

'Fuck sympathy. This is business. Anyhow, I guessed you were all right. They never found your body.'

'So the police have been there?'

'They've been crawling all over the shop for the last couple of days.'

'There now?'

'No. I kept telling them the motor had been nicked off the forecourt, and they finally pretended to believe me.'

'Was my name mentioned?'

'Just in passing. They want you, son, and they want you badly.'

'For fuck's sake. I'm sorry, mate. Put the cleaning or whatever down to me.'

'I will do when I get the sodding thing back. I told you I've got a lot of dough tied up in that motor.'

I lay back on the pillows and said wearily, 'Believe me, I'm as unhappy about it as you are.'

'I just bet you are.'

'I am, mate. Robber's in Intensive Care.'

'I heard. I'm sorry. How come you always come out smelling of roses and your mates get the shitty end of the stick?'

He was right. 'I don't know, Charlie. I really don't. I'll be in touch,' I said, and I switched off the mobile.

I looked at Diane and said, 'I've blown it again.'

'It's not your fault.'

'Yes, it is.'

'Try and get some more sleep.'

'No,' I protested. 'I've slept enough.' But the room darkened and seemed to slip away from me, and I didn't hear her next words although I saw her lips move. Such beautiful lips.

38

I woke up early on Sunday morning feeling a lot better. My forehead still felt tight and painful, but not as tight and painful as before. Diane was asleep next to me and I slid out of bed without disturbing her and made the bathroom without too much effort. Score one for me.

I looked at my wound in the mirror. It was scabbed hard between the stitches, and looked pretty healthy, with little redness or puffiness of the skin where Diane had put the stitches in. This was the first time I'd really looked at it properly and she'd done a good job, pulling the flesh tightly together to minimize scarring later.

I shaved, using the stuff I'd left at her place almost as soon as she moved in, and showered wearing her shower hat to keep the stitches dry. She came into the bathroom as I was towelling myself off and almost bust a gut.

'Very amusing,' I said, gingerly taking off the blue plastic hat decorated with yellow flowers.

'I wish I had a camera.'

'I'm glad you haven't. Fancy going back to bed?'

'Why?' she asked.

'You know.'

'You'll open your wound.'

'There's only one wound I want to open and that's the one between your legs.'

'You south Londoners have such a charming turn of phrase.'

'We're noted for it. So what do you say?'

'Only if you promise to wear my shower cap.'

'Bollocks.'

She grinned. 'Let me clean my teeth and take a pee, and I'll rendezvous with you back under the sheets.'

Later on she went out for the papers and I dressed in the clothes she'd washed and made breakfast. I was feeling much better, especially after exploring Diane's damp patches.

She bought every different newspaper in the shop and by the time we'd finished going through them I had a headache right where I'd been shot, but there was not a single mention of the shooting incident in any of the linens.

'Yesterday's papers,' I said. 'How soon they forget.'

'Just as well.'

'Don't worry. The important ones. The boys in blue haven't forgotten. They hate to be made to look stupid, and I made two of their finest look just that the other night. They'll be on the lookout for me to the max.'

'What are you going to do?'

'How soon can these stitches come out?'

'Let me have a look.'

She examined her handiwork. 'Tomorrow, I should imagine. Or next day at the latest. I just hope I don't make a mess of it. But as it happens the wound's bloody clean. It must be all that practice I've had on your Levis.'

'I always knew the experience would come in handy.' A thought suddenly struck me. 'What are you doing about work, by the way? Sorry. I've been so out of it I forgot to ask. I hope I'm not getting you into trouble.'

'Isn't that what you were just trying to do when we went back to bed?'

144

'Your sense of humour doesn't improve, Diane,' I said. 'So what *are* you doing?'

'I called in on Thursday morning. I had a few days owing and I said a crisis had come up and I needed to take them there and then. They're expecting me back on Wednesday or Thursday this week.'

'Thanks, babe. You're the best. I'll make it up to you.'

'Don't mention it. So what are you going to do? You haven't answered my question.'

'Oh, yeah. Once the stitches are out I'm going to make a social call.'

'Who on?'

'On whom, isn't it? No? Yes?'

'Don't change the subject.'

'Sorry. A geezer I haven't met yet. A certain Mr Tony Lambretta. I think it's time him and me had a chat.'

'Him and I, isn't it?' she said. 'No? Yes?'

39

The stitches came out the next afternoon. Diane used nail scissors with sharp, pointed ends to cut the cotton and was as gentle as she could be, but it still bloody hurt.

I checked the results in the bathroom mirror, and although there was some blood on the tracks, if I let my hair fall forward in a fringe the scar wasn't that noticeable and would improve with time.

That is if I had much time left. Groucho and his boys were still out there and I doubted that they'd mislaid their guns.

But then I hadn't mislaid mine either.

'I need a car,' I said to Diane as we ate supper together.

'Sorry. No can do,' she replied. 'You know I don't have one.'

'Any company cars at work?'

'Nick. No.'

'You won't get involved.'

'I can't.'

'I was only kidding, sweetheart,' I said. 'But your face. No, I'm going to have to steal one.'

'Can you do that?'

'Well, I've got to tell you I'm not the greatest. But I can do it at a pinch. Give me a brick and a screwdriver and I'm your man.'

'Can I come?'

I flashed on Dawn suddenly, and the times she'd helped

me, and what happened to her subsequently, and her best friend, and the baby Dawn was carrying in her belly. Our baby. A little girl who was never to be born but instead would die inside her mother, burnt to death by people we'd made into our enemies.

'No,' I said. 'No chance.'

I'd told her about Dawn, but not the details, and this wasn't the time.

'It's too dangerous,' I added.

'Spoilsport.'

If only she knew.

'Don't worry, darling,' I said. 'I'll be all right.'

'Well, I've always got more needle and thread, I suppose.'

'I wonder how Jack is,' I said. 'I think I'm going to find a phone box and give the hospital a call.'

'Will you be all right?'

'I hope so. But there's only one way to find out.'

'I'm coming with you. I don't want you fainting in some doorway. I imagine it won't be *too* dangerous to walk down the shops with you. In any case, I need a few things.'

'That'd be great,' I said.

Diane had cleaned the blood off my boots and jacket and I put them on. I grabbed her as she was passing and said, 'You're too good to me. I don't deserve it. I could be giving you a ton of grief coming here.'

'Where else would you go?'

'I don't know.'

'Shut up, then. I've enjoyed it. You can't imagine how boring it is working in a finance office all your life. You give me some excitement.'

'Not too much, I hope,' I replied. 'I've seen what's happened to people who've helped me before.'

'I don't care what happens. I'll have the rest of my life to be ordinary.'

And I hope it's a long one, I thought, but said not a word.

We went out of the flat and everything in the street seemed bright after my enforced convalescence, and I was glad Diane was there to hold on to. We cut through some side roads to a shopping parade and I went into a phone box armed with a pile of coins and the hospital number that Diane had given me.

I got through after a couple of minutes of the ringing tone in my ear and asked for Intensive Care. More ringing tone, but just for a few seconds, and a female voice said, 'Intensive Care. Sister speaking.'

'You've got a Jack Robber there,' I said.

'That's right,' she said guardedly, and I wondered if Mr Plod was close by.

'I'm his nephew Bill,' I lied. 'I've been away and I just heard about what happened and I wanted to know how he is.'

I crossed my fingers, almost certain she'd tell me he was in the mortuary.

'He's fine,' she said. 'Of course it'll take time, but we're confident that within a week or so we can release him from ICU, and with any luck he'll be as right as rain in a month or so.'

I breathed out with relief. 'That's great. No chance of a word, I suppose.'

'He's not that much better, I'm afraid,' she said. 'But relatives are welcome. You won't be able to stay long, but at least you can catch a glimpse of him.'

'I'll try,' I said. 'Meanwhile if you can tell him his little nephew from Tulse Hill called . . .'

'I'll do that,' she said.

'Thank you, Sister,' I said, and rang off.

My clothes were damp with sweat, but at least I hadn't been responsible for Jack's death, though I doubted I was going to be very popular with him.

I thought I'd better call Nancy then. I dialled her number from memory and she answered on the third ring. 'Hello, Nance,' I said,

'Nick!' she cried. 'Where the hell have you been? I've had the police here.'

'That's the breaks,' I said. 'Me, I've been on a bed of pain.'

'What happened?'

'Haven't you heard? I thought some of the old Bill would've told you. Robber nearly got killed and I'm in the frame for doing it.'

'That's what they said.'

'Bollocks, love. It was the people who did Harry. And they nearly did for the pair of us as well. I caught a stray shot.'

'Are you all right?'

'I'll survive. But I've had a bad few days. That's why I haven't called before.'

'Where are you?'

'Never you mind. I've got a few things to do. But I'll be around soon. Are you being watched?'

'I don't know. Should I be?'

'Maybe. Listen, I'm going to go now. Don't worry about a thing. Everything's under control. I think I know exactly what's going on. Don't tell anyone I phoned. *Anyone*. I'll be in touch. We'll meet soon and I might be able to answer all your questions. Trust no fucker but me, no matter what they say. Just stay shtuum.'

'God, Nick, I'm so pleased you're all right.'

'Good. And I intend to stay that way. See you later, alligator.' And I hung up on her.

Diane was waiting outside with two carrier bags, and I left the phone box and walked her home. As far as I could see not a single soul was interested in us.

40

I decided to take a ride out to Romford the next day. And when I woke up that morning I felt almost back to my old self. Not that my old self was much to write home about, but I reckoned I'd do.

But first a set of wheels.

'Got a wire coat hanger and a big screwdriver?' I said to Diane after we'd had some breakfast.

'No problem,' she said, went and rooted through the cupboard in the hallway and came up with the tool I wanted. Old, battered and paint-stained as it was. 'There's coat hangers in the wardrobe.'

I went into the bedroom and found a thin wire coat hanger, wrestled it open, doubled it, and pushed it down the sleeve of my jacket. The screwdriver went down the other. To be picked up by some local bobby on the beat as going prepared for theft would be bitterly ironic. But then, I thought, as I put the Detective Special in one jacket pocket, and my phone in the other, that would really be the least of my problems. The Colt was still loaded with five shells, and I had no spares, but then I figured that if I needed more than five shots I was fucked anyway.

I left Diane with a hug and a kiss and a promise to be back later and strolled down to the shops alone. I was potless and withdrew two hundred and fifty quid from the hole in the wall of a branch of my bank, suspecting that it would confirm to the coppers that I was still in the area,

151

but sod that. It was just too bad. They couldn't search every house and flat.

And then I went looking for a nice clean motor.

I walked though the streets of Maida Vale copping a look at the vehicular talent, but every time I thought I might be on a runner there were too many people about. Shit, I thought, as I looked at my watch. This is ridiculous.

Suddenly a male voice from behind me made me jump as it hissed, 'Wanna score?'

I looked round and found a scruffy, dreadlocked boy in dirty jeans and a flowery shirt standing there.

'Do what?' I said.

'I've been watching you. You're looking for something.'

'You're right there.' I had to laugh. No one ever asks me if I want to score these days. I thought I was too old or looked too much like a copper. This boy had to be desperate. 'What you got?'

'Some good charlie.'

I doubted if he'd know good charlie if it jumped up and bit him, but I've been wrong before. Lots of times.

'I might. But I'll need a taste,' I said.

'Come here.' He led me through the covered alley at the side of a block of flats, and I watched for reinforcements who might be up for a quick mugging, but he seemed to be alone.

Once out of the public eye he pulled a thin wrap from his shirt pocket, opened it and offered it to me. Inside was a small quantity of white powder.

I did the old gum test and got a freeze, so I picked up some on my finger and snorted it. Good hit. Good gear. He'd been right.

'How much?' I asked.

'Fifty a gram.'

'All right,' I said. 'I'm game.

I turned away from him and separated fifty from my stash and handed it over. After he counted it, he gave me another slightly fatter wrap.

I tried that too and got the same buzz, and being friendly offered it to him. He grinned and helped himself to a little. 'Cheers,' he said.

Something suddenly occurred to me. The boy seemed like a typical inner city scally, and I said, 'Do you know anyone who nicks motors?'

'Are you serious?' he replied, rubbing his nose.

'Yeah.'

'Me. I can. I used to do it, but it got too dodgy. I kept getting nicked.'

'I'll give you a ton if you can get me one now.'

'I've got no tools.'

'I've got a wire and a screwdriver.'

'You *are* serious.'

'Never more so.'

'Give us. I knew you were looking for something.'

I rescued the tools I'd brought with me from inside my jacket and he said, 'Anything in particular?'

'Something fairly fast and not too obvious.'

'Wait here.' And he turned and walked fast out of the flats.

I lit a Silk Cut and tried to look like I worked for the council. I finished the cigarette and he suddenly popped up again from behind the wall and beckoned me.

I followed him out into the street where a two-litre white Montego was parked at the kerb, engine running. 'Full tank,' he said. 'Who's a lucky boy?'

'Well done,' I said, handed over my last hundred and got behind the wheel.

153

The screwdriver and wire were on the passenger seat, the ignition was busted and wires sprouted from the steering column, but otherwise everything was kosher.

I ran down the electric window and he said, 'Stall it to stop the engine and touch the red and blue wires there' – he pointed to the steering column – 'to start it again. But be careful – you can get a nasty shock.'

'Cheers,' I said. 'Are you often about?'

'Most of the time.'

'What's your name?'

'Cedric. People call me Ricky.'

'I'm Nicholas. People call me Nick. I might be able to put some work your way in the future, Ricky.'

'There's a café in the square,' he said, pointing vaguely over the top of the flats. 'Bunter's, it's called. Fucking silly name. But I hang around there sometimes. Just ask for Ricky.'

'I might just do that,' I said, put the car into gear and pulled away.

41

So there I was in a stolen car with an illegal firearm and a gram of coke. I felt a bit like Clyde without Bonnie. But I'd had a chance to drag my Bonnie along and passed on it.

At the first set of lights I took out the wrap, opened it and stuck a quarter of the contents up my hooter. I got a hit big time. About as big time as you could get without blowing the top off your head. Maybe this was going to be fun after all. And if I survived it I was definitely going to look up Ricky again.

I got to Romford, got lost, found myself, and eventually arrived at the estate where Robber and I had seen Groucho go into The Laurels. I drove around aimlessly for half an hour and then found the house itself. It took me a lot longer than it might, because every so often I was taking a toot of charlie and I was a bit disorientated. Maybe not the way to go into a potentially lethal situation, but if I'd've been straight I might never have gone in at all.

I steered the Montego down a lane that seemed to go round the back of the house's grounds and drove it into a thicket away from the prying eyes of the security firm and stalled it to a halt.

I took myself, the last of my coke and my gun out for a stroll, and I felt like the last man with legs left in Essex as the only other humans I'd seen were well insulated inside tons of shiny metal.

I went right round the grounds of the house, looking for

an easy way in. Finally I saw that the branch of one of the trees at the back of the property hung over the wall then dipped down until it almost touched the knee-high grass at the side of the lane. Nought out of ten for the tree surgeons involved.

I swung myself up through the leaves and worked myself gingerly along until I had passed over the wall and could just see the back of the house through the thick foliage. I dropped down on to the ground and froze for a minute or so. I'd been in close proximity to dogs before, and the last thing I wanted to meet right then was a pair of half-starved Dobermanns looking for their dinner. In other words, me.

But all was quiet and I moved through the undergrowth until I could see the lawns and flower beds leading up to the tennis courts, swimming pool, and patio area at the back of the house.

Nice bit of real estate, I thought, and compared it with my slightly bigger than a studio, one-room flat. And they say that crime doesn't pay.

Talking of crime, I took the coke out of my pocket and snorted up the last of the gram, screwed up the wrap and risked a fine by littering the path right in front of me.

Desperado!

I skirted the path and made towards Tony Lambretta's country seat, keeping as close to the bushes and trees as I could.

No one was having a quick couple of sets after an early lunch, and no one was splashing in the water.

Not that they couldn't have. Like the garden, the courts were immaculate and the water in the pool looked so clean and fresh I was tempted to take a dip myself.

But right then I was more interested in seeing if there were any guards armed with semi-automatic weapons.

But all was serene. God was in his heaven and all was right with Tony Lambretta's little world.

I decided to see if I could change all that.

I stepped softly on to the patio and looked at the blank windows facing me. Not a sign of a soul. I crept up to the patio doors and made a mask with my hand so that I could see through to the other side.

No one.

Good, I thought, and tried the sliding door. It opened as smoothly and quietly as if it had just been oiled.

Better and better.

At least that proved there was someone home.

I stepped through the doorway and into some interior designer's idea of a swinging pad for the middle to late nineties, all leather, suede and chrome with framed posters on the wall and a huge wet bar down one side, with captain's chairs fixed to the marble floor on their swivelling bases.

Cool, I thought, business must be good, when someone stuck what felt suspiciously like the muzzle of a gun into my kidney.

42

'I'll take that,' a male voice whispered in my ear, and a hand appeared around one side of me and took the cocked Colt out of my fist. Simple as that. No problems. But then I've got this strange attachment to my internal organs and fancied keeping them for a bit yet. 'Move over there,' the voice continued, and I walked forward slowly. 'Hands away from the body.'

I did as I was told.

'You made me jump,' I said for something to say, and to keep whoever's finger off the trigger.

'Turn round,' said the voice, and I did as I was told again, and a geezer I'd never seen before was standing there. He was thirtyish, medium height, medium build, nothing much facially, with dark thinning hair, a dark suit and a white shirt. Mr Average.

'We've been watching you on the video,' he said. 'Who are you?'

'Boy's Brigade. Collecting for new instruments for the band. It's unorthodox, I know, but we try new things all the time.'

You could tell he wasn't amused, and he let down the hammer of the Colt and slid it into his pocket with his left hand. His right was busy with a 9mm Browning Hi-Power.

'Who the fuck are you making jokes?' shouted an angry voice from behind me. I looked round, and an older, fatter, balder, greasier bloke dressed in nothing less than two grands' worth of Bond Street Italian designer style came waddling in. He was also shorter than the other geezer, and frankly the wide trousers he was wearing didn't flatter his little legs.

'I got the gun he was carrying, Mr L,' said Mr Average. 'But I ain't searched him yet.'

'Do it, then,' said Mr L. Tony Lambretta as I lived and breathed. But for how much longer? I wondered.

Mr Average gave Lambretta the Browning, moved round carefully so as not to get in the line of fire, and gave me a brief but thorough search. He found my wallet in my hip pocket. When he put his hand up to my groin, I said, 'You should work at Burton's. You'd enjoy it.'

'Shut the fuck up!' screamed Lambretta.

Sense of humour bypass.

Me. After all that coke I could see the funny side of it. After all that coke I could see the funny side of the Holocaust.

'He's clean,' said Mr Average, straightening up and taking my gun out of his pocket.

'Who the hell are you to come to my house with a gun?' said Tony Lambretta, his voice a little calmer.

'*You've* got guns,' I said.

'This is *my* house.'

I said nothing.

'What if my kids had been out at the pool?'

Nothing.

'You would've killed one, maybe?'

I shook my head at that. 'No, Mr Lambretta,' I said. 'But I might've taken one hostage.'

He kicked me then, running forward and trying to land one in my groin, I turned slightly and took it on my thigh. But it still hurt like fuck.

'His name is Sharman, boss,' said Mr Average after checking around my credit cards.

'Sharman,' said Lambretta with barely controlled fury. 'He's the bastard's been sticking his nose in with that fucker Robber.'

'We just never learn,' I said mildly.

'You're dead, you fucker,' said Lambretta his finger tightening on the trigger. 'Dead. Just like your friend'll be when we get hold of him.'

'We've all gotta go some time,' I said.

'I'll get Jules over here,' said Lambretta to Mr Average. 'You lock this piece of shit away upstairs till we need him. Make sure he stays there.'

Jules. Groucho. Shit.

Mr Average poked me hard in the ribs and gestured that I should precede him. I did. Out of the room and up a wide flight of stairs like something out of *Gone With the Wind* to the first floor, then along the hall. When we got to a room at the end he said, 'Inside,' and I just knew he was going to give me a whack on the head.

No more, I thought. I've had enough of head wounds. If he hit me from behind I'd be bound to fall on my healing wound, and if I turned he'd hit me at the front, and either way I might end up with my brain spilling out of my skull. Three days I'd been out of it the last time. Who knew how long it might be before I came round if I got hit again? If ever.

But turn I did, and Mr Average looked at me, the Colt pointing at my abdomen. He hadn't cocked it so it was on double action. Just a fraction of a second slower to fire than if he'd cocked the hammer. And it's so easy to miss with a small handgun, even at close range. A centimetre of move-ment of the muzzle end could mean a foot or more at mine.

160

It was worth the risk. The worst that could happen was that I'd end up dead. And the coke made me fearless.

'It's unloaded,' I said.

I knew he hadn't checked it, and for one brief second he believed me and looked down at the gun in his hand. It wavered, and I did exactly what his boss had tried to do to me. I kicked him so hard in the nuts that I expected his bollocks to pop out of his mouth.

Man, but that speed made me fast.

The pain paralysed his trigger finger just like I'd prayed it would. He gave me one agonized look, made a strangled cry, and fell to the thick carpet with hardly a sound, the gun bouncing off the pile in front of him.

Then I kicked him in the head just to make sure.

43

I went through his pockets and found my wallet, then I found his. His name was John Duncan. He had a wodge of large denomination notes and a bunch of credit cards, so I nicked the lot. Then I tied his hands behind him with the silk tie he was wearing. I pulled it so tight that I heard the stitches rip and I knew that even a trip down Sketchley's wouldn't put Humpty together again. I hoped it had been expensive.

I cocked the Colt and crept downstairs, where I could hear Lambretta holding a one-sided conversation with the phone. I waited until he hung up before walking back into the room overlooking the patio. Lambretta was gazing out over the garden away from me; the Browning was on the top of the bar maybe ten feet from where he was standing. Perfect. He heard my footsteps on the marble and said, thinking I was Duncan, 'You got the bastard sorted?'

'He's sorted all right, Mr Lambretta, but I think we're talking about different bastards. Now just keep your hands where I can see them.'

He spun round and I showed him my gun before walking over and picking up the automatic and putting it in my pocket. 'What the f—?' he said.

I winked at him. 'Can't get the staff these days, can you?'

His eyes went to the door.

'No. He won't be down.'

'You cunt.'

'Granted. Are we alone?'

Lambretta nodded and I believed him. 'Jules is coming,' he said.

'He'll be a while. And I won't be stopping. But before I go you can answer me a couple of questions.'

'What questions? I ain't answering any questions. Fuck you.'

'Then I'll shoot you and leave you for Jules to find. I don't give a shit, Tone. I'm wanted for attempted murder and lots more, thanks to you and your mates. If I'm going down I might as well go down for something I *did* do.'

He didn't say much to that. Could've been due to the fact that by then I was foaming at the mouth from the coke. I must've looked like a rabid dog seeing a pond full of water.

'Are you carrying by, the way?' I asked.

'No.'

'Because you've got such a great minder, is it? I'd think again. But just for the record slip off your jacket.'

He did as he was told. I could see no sign of a gun. 'Pull up your trouser legs,' I said.

'Do what?'

'Just in case you're wearing an ankle holster.'

'For fuck's sake,' he said, but he did as I told him. Nothing.

'Good enough,' I said. 'So why did you kill Harry Stonehouse?'

'Who?'

'*Don't piss me off!*' I screamed. 'I know you done it.'

'That bitch—' he said, but cut himself off and clamped his mouth tight shut.

'What bitch?' I asked. But I could guess.

163

He shook his head, but he'd partway answered my question.

'Where's the money?' I asked.

'What money?'

'The money from the 4F security van blag. Twenty million in old notes. That money.'

'I don't know what you're talking about.'

I squeezed the trigger and the Colt jumped in my hand, and more by luck than judgement a plaster bust of Elvis from the Vegas era that was standing on a tall chiffonier about three feet from where he was standing exploded into powder.

'You're fucking mad,' he said in the aftermath of the shot.

'Fucking mad,' I said. 'And getting madder by the second. So tell me about the money.'

'There's no money here.'

'I didn't expect you'd keep it under the mattress,' I said. 'But you've got it, ain't you?'

He seemed to regain his confidence then, as if I'd asked the wrong question. 'You going to kill me?' he said.

And crazy as I was, I wasn't. Going to kill him, that is, much as I might want to, and I think he knew it.

'Not today,' I said.

'You'd better piss off, then,' he said. 'Jules won't be on his own.'

He had some bottle, I'd give him that, and he was right. I didn't fancy a gun fight. And besides, the shot had given me a headache right on my scar.

'Yeah,' I said. 'And you're going to walk me to my car. Come on.' I knew I'd been at the right place, but this was the wrong time. I wanted to go and have a think. Regroup and marshal my forces, however pathetic they were.

I walked over, grabbed Lambretta by the shoulder and shoved him out into the hall. 'How do the front gates open?' I said.

He pointed to a console covered in buttons by the front door. 'Go on, then,' I ordered.

He walked over and pressed one. It could've been a panic button for the security firm that toured the area but I doubted it. I didn't think Lambretta wanted any witnesses. 'Door,' I said.

He opened the wide front door and together we walked down the drive. The gates stood open and I held the gun tight to my side as I made him walk with me to where I'd left the Montego.

I got in and touched the wires together just like Ricky had said and the engine started first go.

I reversed out from the undergrowth and turned the car round, then let the window down and for the first time he looked scared, as if I might just shoot and run.

'I'll be seeing you again,' I said. 'Count on it.' And I slammed my foot down on the accelerator, fishtailing the car away, and shooting dirt and grit over his flash whistle.

44

On the way back to town I decided I'd really fucked that one up. I'd need more time with Lambretta. Much more time. And some kind of leverage. I could've taken him with me, I supposed, but where? I had nowhere to go. I could hardly take him back to Diane's with me. That would've pleased her no end. Having Tony Lambretta as a reluctant lodger.

I suppose I could've shot him, but what would've been the point? At least I was damned sure Robber had been right in his hypothesis. And alive Tony Lambretta could lead me to the cash and what really happened to Harry Stonehouse on his ten months away. Dead, he'd've been no use to me at all.

I skirted the West End and headed towards Fulham. On the way I keyed Nancy Stonehouse's number into my portable. She answered quickly. 'Are you alone?' I asked.

'Nick. Thank God. Yes, of course I'm alone.'

There was no of course about it, but I let it go. 'Is the house being watched?' I asked.

'I don't know. Should it be?'

'It wouldn't surprise me. Got your car?'

'Yes.'

'Right. Get in and drive over the river. Go to Barnes. There's a pub there called the Rising Sun. Right in the middle of the village. Meet me there in half an hour. Make sure you're not followed.'

'This all sounds a little melodramatic.'

'*Melodramatic*,' I said. 'Robber's in hospital with three bullet holes in him. I get a face full of lead, and . . . Listen, I'll tell you all about it when we meet. Just make sure if anyone follows you you lose them. If you can't, go back home and I'll call you later. Don't, whatever you do, let anyone come after you to the pub or I'm in deep shit.'

'OK, Nick,' she said in a chastened tone.

I was at the boozer within fifteen minutes and stuck the car on a meter opposite the pub although there was a big car park at the back. Whatever Nancy thought, there was a chance someone could be watching and I didn't rate her as a stoppo driver. So I sat in the car and watched the pub, although I was dying for a drink.

She turned up dead on time, drove round the back of the building and I checked the cars that came after her. No one seemed interested and I watched as she came round the front again and went into the bar. I reckoned she was clean, so I left the Montego, stuck half a quid in the meter like a law-abiding citizen, and went into the boozer after her.

She was sitting at a table with a drink in front of her. 'Hello,' I said.

'There *was* some sod watching the house,' she said and my stomach did a somersault.

'What kind of car?'

'Black Ford, I think.'

A black Ford. Could be the good guys or the bad guys. But at least it proved someone was still interested.

'I left him this side of the bridge when I did an illegal U-turn,' Nancy went on. 'Last seen fuming between a bus and a post office van.'

'Are you sure?'

''Course I am. I know it round here. There's lots of little streets to get lost in. Don't worry, I made sure.'

There'd been no black Fords following her, I was sure of that. 'Great,' I said, and nodded at her drink. 'You all right?'

'Another gin'd be good.'

'I thought it might,' I said, and went to the bar and got myself a pint and a large Vera for the lady, as the barman put it.

When I was sat down with a quarter of the pint inside me and a cigarette lit, I said, 'Know a face called Tony Lambretta?'

I could tell by her eyes that she did. 'Who?' she said.

Bad sign.

'Lambretta,' I said. 'Like the motor scooter.'

She shook her head.

I leant over, took her wrist and squeezed it hard. 'Nancy,' I said. 'I know you. I know lots about you. I've seen the little birth mark on your thigh. I've even kissed it. Now don't fuck about with me, there's a good girl, or I'll break your fucking wrist.'

She twisted her hand away and I saw that the barman had noticed. I smiled an all boys together smile, hoping he'd think it was just a little domestic about the price of peas or something. He grinned back and resumed polishing a glass. We men have to stick together in the battle of the sexes.

'There's no need to threaten me,' she said.

'I think there is. I nearly got killed the other night.' I moved my hair to let her clearly see the healing scar. 'So did my mate. Now I want to know exactly what's going on. Thanks for your show of concern, by the way.'

She frowned. 'I'm sorry, Nick. It's just that I'm not used to all this.'

'Get used to it,' I said. 'I don't think the fat lady's going to be singing for a bit. This one won't be over till it's over, and something tells me we've hardly started yet.'

Her frown deepened and she lit one of my cigarettes. 'Shit,' she said. 'I suppose I'd better tell you everything.'

'Good idea.' I lit another cigarette myself and yawned. The speed was still inside me, but I recognized signs of a crash coming.

'God,' she said again. 'This is difficult. I haven't been exactly honest with you.'

'You amaze me.'

'Are you going to listen or what?'

'I'll listen.'

So she told me.

45

'I don't know where to start, really.'

'The beginning is usually good.'

'It's not as easy as that. Where does one thing end and another begin?'

I shrugged and hoped the conversation wasn't going to get too Zen-like.

'I told you that Harry and I were leading separate lives at the end.'

I nodded.

'Well *I* was, but Harry was still in love with me. There'd been other men . . .'

I knew that too. Obviously. I'd been one of them. 'Lots?' I asked. I didn't want to, but I had to. No one wants to be seen as just one of a crowd.

She guessed my reasons for asking. 'Not a lot. A few. I didn't screw the milkman and the bloke who came to read the electricity meter if that's what you're thinking.'

That was exactly what I'd been thinking, but I said nothing.

'Did Harry know?' I asked.

She nodded.

'All of them?'

'Most.'

'Did he know about me?'

She nodded again.

'When it was going on?'

'Probably. We were never exactly discreet, were we?'

'Shit,' I said. And he'd kept phoning to invite me to meet him for a drink. Poor fucker.

'He didn't care,' she said. 'No, that's not true. Of course he cared. He loved me. But he'd forgive me anything. That's why I never left. I never found anyone better. It was easy with Harry. I did what I liked and he accepted that.'

It sounded as cold and lonely as hell to me. Because I reckon that if there is a hell it's not hot like they say in the Bible. I imagine it would be as cold as the inside of a freezer. And dark. And you'd always be alone so that you could consider what you'd done to end up there.

She stopped and took a drink and lit another of my cigarettes.

'I know where he was for that time,' she said eventually.

And I suppose that was when I stopped liking Nancy Stonehouse.

'You what?' I said.

'I lied to you. I know where he was for the time he went missing.'

'Where?'

'He was in a witness-protection programme.'

Robber had been dead right.

'Jesus, Nancy,' I said. 'You've made a right fucking fool out of me.'

'No. Listen.'

'I'm listening.'

'He was involved in that big robbery at 4F.'

'You amaze me.'

'They got away with twenty million.'

'I'm aware of the figures.'

'The police kept on at him. Him doing the job he did.

171

He knew all about the lorry's route and the radio codes. They never let him alone.'

'They tend to do that.'

'He was at his wits' end. Being in the job for so long gives you a different perspective. You don't understand what it's like to be on the other side of the law.'

I do, I thought.

'And in the end he told them everything. He informed on the men who did it. At least the ones he knew about. It was all planned so that only one or two people knew everyone involved. Very professional.'

'And they got nicked.'

'The ones he told about, and then some of the ones that got arrested informed on others. If you see what I mean.'

'I see. And the rest went off to Spain.'

'Some of them. Some of them stayed. The unimportant ones on the periphery. And some of the planners Harry didn't even know about. There were a lot of people in on it.'

'And you knew all about it.'

'Not then. Afterwards. After he vanished.'

'How?'

'He came back.'

'He was just doing it part time, you mean? The witness protection. Like a Saturday job?'

'That's right. He told me that he couldn't leave me. Not for good.'

'So why didn't he take you with him? Into witness protection, I mean.'

'I don't know ... Oh, I do. I was having another affair. This time I thought it was for real. He thought it would be the perfect time to make a clean break. But he couldn't stay away.'

'So he blew his cover.'

'Yes. And then he was grabbed.'

'By Lambretta?'

'That's right. He was one of the planners. The police knew about him but they couldn't prove anything. I think they pulled him in a couple of times. But they had to let him go. He's got friends. Important friends.'

'I imagine he would have. So why didn't you tell the police? After Harry turned up, I mean. Why involve me?'

She licked her lips, stubbed out her cigarette and lit another one straight away.

'The money,' she said.

I had a horrible feeling I knew what was coming next.

'What about the money?' I said.

'It was never recovered, and Harry knew where it was. That was part of his job. Keeping it safe until the split.'

'He had all the money?'

'That's right.'

'And he didn't give it up when he informed on his fellow criminals.'

She nodded.

'And when they eventually found him they tortured him for it.'

Another nod.

'This doesn't make sense,' I said. 'Unless . . .'

'Unless?' she said.

'Unless he fell in with some bent coppers.'

She made a face.

'Bell?'

She nodded yet again and I had a flash of intuition.

'He wouldn't by any chance be the bloke you were having it off with – the one you thought was the real thing?'

173

Yet another nod.

'Christ, Nancy,' I said. 'What the fuck were you playing at?'

She shrugged this time.

'And why are you telling me now?'

'I split with Phil. Philip Bell. He wasn't the person I thought he was.'

'They so rarely are. But wait a minute. I'm confused. How did Lambretta suss him out? Find him, I mean.'

'I don't know. He got careless, I suppose. The stupid wanker.'

'He was your husband.'

'What husband? He was no husband to me. He was weak. You were more of a husband to me than he ever was.'

'You bitch.'

'No. I deserved something for all the time I wasted with him.'

'But you *did* get something, didn't you? You told me you had money when you first got me involved. I should've fucking known.'

'It was peanuts compared with what they got away with in that robbery. Chickenfeed.'

'So you just sent me in blind to see what I could see, and to fuck with the consequences.'

'Nick. I'm sorry.'

'Sorry. So you fucking should be.' I could hear the tone of my voice rising and I stopped. The barman was looking at me oddly again. I had to be careful.

'I didn't know what to tell you,' she said pleadingly.

'Lies. Obviously. Like everything else you've told me.'

46

'So let me get this straight,' I said, when I'd got another couple of drinks and some cigarettes from the machine, and I'd felt Nancy's eyes on me for every second I was absent from the table. 'Lambretta knew Harry when he was in the job. Correct?'

'That's right.'

'And after Harry went to 4F, Lambretta put some pressure on him to supply information about the transport of old notes.'

'Anything valuable, really. Gold bullion. Cash. Anything.'

'So why did Harry give in? He was known for being straight.'

'He didn't at first. He just laughed at Lambretta. Then later he wanted money too. He wanted the pair of us to start again. A new life.'

'And he would need a lot of dough for that, wouldn't he?'

She nodded. I didn't think that Nancy spoke or understood irony.

'To keep you in the manner you could fast become accustomed to.'

Another nod.

'But you were having it off with Bell.'

Yet another.

'It all comes back to you, doesn't it, Nancy? Every time,' I said.

'It's not my fault.'

''Course not.'

'I wasn't getting any younger, Nick.'

'But a minute ago you told me you knew nothing about it until after the event.'

'Maybe I had a rough idea.'

'Maybe you did. Was it because he really thought he was going to lose you that time? To DI Bell?'

'Maybe.'

'You turned into a real charmer, didn't you?'

'You can talk.'

And of course she was correct.

'So why me, Nancy? Why pick on me?'

'I was at my wits' end until I thought of you. You're a loose cannon. I knew you'd do something.'

'And of course I owed Harry, and myself. As you so accurately put it.'

'Right.'

'So what we have here is a bunch of East End villains, a gang of bikers . . .'

'What? What bikers?' she said.

'Don't worry about it, I'll explain later. A bent copper. By the way, was he in it on his own or did he have help?'

'He had help.'

'Not a nasty little Welshman named Graham Jackson? All muscle, including between his ears.'

'Yes,' she said. 'That sounds like him.'

'This gets better,' I said. 'So. There's the villains, the bikers, the bent coppers, Harry and you, and now me and Jack Robber all chasing twenty million in old notes.'

'That's about the strength of it,' she agreed. 'But I don't know anything about the bikers.'

'They got rid of your weak little hubby's body. Don't give it a second thought.'

'Don't be angry, Nick.'

'Angry. Who, me? Out of the question. I love being lied to and shot at. So where is the dosh now? Does anyone know?'

'I'm sure someone does. But not me.'

'I reckon it's your ex-mate Philip Bell. That's why Mr Lambretta was so short with me.'

'When?'

'Earlier today when I paid him a visit.'

'You've *seen* Tony Lambretta?'

'Too fucking right I have. But I don't think I'm going to be number one on his Christmas card list.'

'What happened?'

'Not a lot. But I suspect he hasn't seen much of the missing money. He was a trifle miffed about the whole deal.'

'And what are you going to do about it?'

'Get it back.'

'And then?'

'And then spend it.'

'See, Nick, you're not that much different to me, are you?'

'Not a lot.' And I wasn't proud of it. But maybe, just maybe I could do something about it if it wasn't too late. And then it struck me. Harry had kept calling. I wondered if it was because he wanted to reach out to me. To tell me what he'd got himself into. And that made me feel worse if anything.

'What about me?' she asked after a second.

'Don't worry, Nancy. You'll get what you deserve.'

Exactly what she deserved. I planned to make it my business.

'So what are you going to do?'

177

'Have a word with a few people.'

'Who?'

'Don't worry your pretty little head, love. You let me take care of that. Now you're going home and I'm going . . . Well, to where I can lay my head. I'll be in touch. Stay close to the phone. I might need you in a hurry. OK?'

'OK.'

'Good. Now scarper. I've got things to think about.'

And she did. Without another word.

Cunt, I thought as she left.

47

I left soon after myself. I nodded at the barman as I went. He nodded back. I went over the road, rescued the Montego and headed for Diane's place.

On the way I started to formulate a plan. I was due to make some restitution. To Harry, to Robber, and last but not least, to myself.

I was really crashing from the coke by then, smoking one cigarette after another until my throat was raw, and chewing at the inside of my mouth until it bled. And although it was still reasonably early I knew I was just about finished for the day.

I left the car close to where I'd met Ricky and walked back towards Diane's. My mouth was bone dry and I dropped into a little boozer on a back street, bought a pint and took a fresh packet of cigarettes to a table at the back where the lights were dim, and thought about what I'd learned.

As far as I could see, Tony Lambretta didn't have the stolen money, so there was no point in putting any more pressure on him right now, and besides, next time I might not be as lucky as I had been to get away with my skin in one piece. But he wanted it, and maybe I could use his greed against him. He'd had Robber and me shot, and he was due to pay for that.

The bikers were just soldiers. Thick, and out of their heads on drugs and booze. They probably didn't know what sodding day it was, but they might end up being useful if I could turn them against Lambretta and his gang.

Nancy was just a stupid bitch with an eye for the main chance, who'd been used by everyone and had decided to try and use me. Well, that was all over, and her time was near.

No, it had to be DI Bell and his little firm who knew where the dough was stashed. Bastards. Playing both ends against the middle and getting friends of mine killed and hurt in the process. Their time was near too. DS Graham Jackson. I had old scores to settle with that little bastard, and something told me, muscles or not, he was the weak link in the chain.

I finished my pint and half a dozen more Silk Cut and went out and took the long way round to Diane's, making sure no one clocked my progress.

She was inside waiting for me, and I told her what had occurred.

'You're the only one apart from me who knows the whole story,' I said. 'At least the only one I can trust. If anything happens to me, I want you to blow the whistle. Will you do that?'

'Yes, Nick. But for God's sake be careful.'

'Careful,' I said as I started to nod out on the sofa, another cigarette between my fingers. 'That's my middle name.'

48

I woke up alone, still on the sofa, with a duvet slung over me. It was five in the morning.

I went through to the bathroom, scoping the bedroom in passing. Diane was under the covers with her face in the pillow and her thick hair spread out like a fan. I carried on, took a piss and blew my nose on some loo paper. There was plenty of blood in the mix, and I had that weird feeling that I was still speeding, although I'd slept for hours. That'd teach me.

I went back through the flat to the kitchen, put on the kettle for tea and lit a cigarette.

It tasted like shit and I put it out under the tap and dropped it in the garbage.

I drank my tea looking out of the window as London woke up, shook itself, and got ready for a new day.

Then I made more tea, took two cups into the bedroom and got into bed. 'What do you want?' said Diane sleepily.

'A fuck would be nice.'

'Think again,' she said. 'I've got my period and I don't want the sheets messing.'

'Thanks for sharing that thought.'

'Share some thoughts with me. What are you going to do next?'

'Kidnap a copper, I think,' I said. 'Give him the fright of his life and see what pops out.'

'You're going to get into serious trouble.'

'I'm already in serious sodding trouble. What more can happen?'

'You could get killed.'

'There's always that, I suppose.'

'Nick. When will you ever learn?'

'Listen. It was you insisted I got involved with Nancy Stonehouse in the first place. And as soon as I do, you accuse me of having it away with her, and now you're telling me I should quit. Well, I can't. I'm in this up to my bloody ears and that's all there is to it.'

'OK, Nick, OK. Have it your own way.'

My own way. Women! Fuck me. What planet do they come from? As an old mate used to say to me: Can't live with them. Can't live with them.

And so I *had* screwed Nancy. But own up, she had blind-sided me. I more or less just lay there and thought of England.

'I need another sodding car,' I said after a bit. 'Fuck me, it's easier to buy them.'

49

We both dropped off again and woke up about lunchtime. Diane got up and made some breakfast whilst I washed and shaved.

I went into the kitchen for egg, bacon, sausage and tomato.

'Feeling better?' she asked.

'Do you know that my mum used to cut the whites off fried eggs for me?' I said.

'You're feeling better. And your mum won't give you a blow job.'

'Nor will you if this morning's performance was anything to go by.'

'I was tired.'

'And having your time of the month. Well, I suppose if you've got to suffer I've got to as well. How long does it usually last, by the way?' We'd never been in such close proximity for any length of time before.

'A week of PMTs, and a week of period usually.'

'Jesus. Do you realize that that's a fortnight out of every month? Half your life you go round with a pain in your belly.'

'Yes, I do, thanks. It's not my fault I'm one of those rare women with delicate insides.'

'Not so rare,' I remarked. 'I always seem to end up with them. Just my luck, I suppose.'

'Nick. You are seriously asking for a smack.'

'No. I might enjoy it too much, and that would never do.'

'Bollocks.'

I grinned and chewed on a piece of bacon. Game, set and match to me, I think.

She sat and drank a mug of tea and looked at me over the rim. 'Got a plan yet?' she said.

'Sure.'

'About getting another car.'

'It's in the bag.'

'Brick and screwdriver? Or are you going to find . . . Whassisname . . . ? Ricky again?'

'No. Simpler than that. Got a cross-head screwdriver and a pair of pliers?'

'I think so.'

'I love a girl who does DIY.'

'Woman.'

'Sorry. Did I say something wrong there? Did I lose PC points or what?'

'What's the matter with you today?'

'Shit. I dunno. Sorry, doll. Or is doll not allowed either?'

'Doll'll do.' And she grinned, and I grinned back, so that was all right.

First thing after the dishes were done was that I phoned Denmark Hill nick from a different phone box from the one I'd used before. 'Is Graham Jackson in?' I asked the voice that answered the phone.

'I haven't seen him. I'll put you through to CID.'

A female voice answered after three rings. 'CID. DC Vernon speaking.'

'Is Graham in today?' I said. 'Graham Jackson?'

'He's on late turn today,' she replied. 'Can I help?'

'No, love, it's all right. It's personal. Will you tell him John called?'

'John who?'

'Just John. He'll know.'

She knew better than to delve further. 'Certainly. I'll tell him.'

''Bye,' I said.

''Bye.' And we hung up.

Chances are she'd forget. But even if she didn't, John's a common name. Graham Jackson was bound to know half a dozen at least.

'I'll be going out later,' I said to Diane when I got back to her flat.

'So we've got time to go back to bed.'

'What about the sheets?'

'Fuck the sheets.'

'I'd rather fuck you.'

And I did.

Round about five I took a walk, taking the tools I needed, and giving Diane a farewell kiss. I won't tell you where. It looked like her fortnight was up, and mine was just about to begin.

I went over towards the Edgware Road, looking for a decent car on a meter with just a short time to run. After half an hour I found a late model, silver BMW 7-series with about ten minutes on it. I stood in the doorway of a mansion block near the meter, lit a cigarette and wondered if the driver was a law-abiding citizen.

He was. Just as the meter was about to click over to 'Penalty' he came back. He was short, olive-skinned, wearing a smart suit and carrying a snakeskin briefcase. He clicked off the alarm on the BMW as he approached it, and its lights flashed three times in surrender.

I met him by the car, just an ordinary geezer taking a stroll. 'Nice motor,' I said.

He looked at me like I'd just exposed myself to his wife. 'Mmm,' he replied.

'Easy to drive?' I asked.

'Excuse me, I've got an appointment.'

I checked the street. No one was looking. 'You're going to be late,' I said, and took out the Browning niner that was in my pocket.

'What?' he spluttered as I took the car keys out of his hand.

'Shit happens. You got a portable phone?'

He was too flabbergasted to lie. 'In my case,' he said.

I took that off him too. 'Thanks,' I said. 'Don't worry, I'll take care of it. Might even put some petrol in. Unleaded, is it?'

He nodded as I threw the case in the back, got in, closed the door, ran down the window and started the car. 'Cheers,' I said as I pulled away and winked at him.

I drove straight to Euston Station underground car park. It's big and anonymous, and full of pretty nice motors, and within two minutes I found another Beemer of the same year and switched the plates. I was out of the car park within ten minutes and turned the car south.

50

I got caught in the rush hour, but I wasn't in any hurry and just sat in the BMW with the air-conditioning on and a tape of Motown hits of the sixties in the machine. The geezer I'd nicked the car off had better taste in music than I'd've given him credit for. Mind you, the rest of the music in the glove compartment was the usual AOR dreck you'd expect.

All the time I'd worn a pair of black leather gloves I'd borrowed from Diane. They were far too small, almost cutting off the circulation, and made my hands sweat bullets. But I didn't want to leave any prints and they sort of made me feel like Robert Vaughn in *The Magnificent Seven*. Then I remembered that he was the first one to get killed, which spoiled my mood a little.

I got to Denmark Hill around seven, seven-fifteen, and put the motor in the car park of the Fox On the Hill and went inside for a drink. It was on the other side of the area from the nick and as far as I remembered not a favourite for the coppers who worked there to drink in.

At least I didn't recognize anyone.

On the way I peeled off the gloves. I didn't want anyone to remember anything eccentric about me.

I'd bought a paper from a boy risking his life in the traffic on the journey down, and I sat in the pub all evening filling myself with Dutch courage.

A drunken driving charge was the least of my worries right then.

About half an hour before closing time I rescued the motor and drove round to the nick. If young Graham was about, there was a chance he'd go out in time for last orders.

I was in luck. As I sat opposite the station where I could see both the back and front entrances, he came out with an older geezer I didn't recognize. Probably his DI, unless Graham had gone bent and was in a serious homosexual relationship with a father figure.

Hey, listen. In this life, I've found anything is possible.

They got into a Ford Sierra, Graham Jackson taking the wheel, and drove away. I followed. They didn't go far. Just about a quarter of a mile to a pub called the Standing Man. Graham put the car in the small car park at the rear and they vanished inside. I parked opposite where once again I could see all the bar entrances and waited.

At eleven a battered Vauxhall with a radio aerial arrived and collected the older man. At twenty past the last few punters were ejected and the lights inside were dimmed, but there was no sign of my quarry.

A bit of afters, I thought. You coppers. You'll be the death of me.

I sat there till sodding 2 a.m. rubbing life into my hands through the thin gloves before the back door opened and Graham Jackson weaved his way across the car park to his motor.

He was alone.

I was close behind. It must've been my day for car-jacking. I left the keys in the BMW. Either for the coppers, or so that no one would have to damage the motor if they lifted it.

Jackson found *his* keys and bent down to locate the door lock.

I moved in behind him and as he opened the driver's door I clocked him one hard with the butt of the Browning just behind his left ear.

I caught him as he fell and just managed to hold him up long enough to flick up the lock on the back door, open it, and push him inside.

'There you go, Graham,' I said to his prone body as I shoved his feet inside and closed the door quietly before taking the keys out of the door where he'd left them. 'Welcome to your worst-case scenario.'

51

There's one good thing about that part of London. You're never very far from somewhere dark and quiet. I found just the place at the back of a burnt-out row of shops. Maybe the leaseholder couldn't make the mortgage and did a bit of do-it-yourself remodelling with a petrol can to get the insurance.

And maybe I'm getting cynical in my old age.

I swung the car round, killed the engine, got out of the front, opened the back door and checked Graham Jackson out. He was still in the land of nod and snoring gently. Of course, I was so unprepared I had nothing to tie him up with. So I opened the hatchback of the car and in the splash of light from the high beams I found a piece of what looked like speaker wire and fastened his hands together tightly behind his back. I'd hoped to find some handcuffs, but there's never a copper about when you need one, so I had to improvise. In the front well of the car was an unopened can of Coke. I sprung the tab and poured the liquid over Graham Jackson's face. He came awake spluttering and coughing as he almost drowned in the Real Thing.

'Hello, Graham,' I said, leaning over from the front seat where I was sitting, the automatic in my hand. 'How's the head?'

'Are you mad?' he said, shaking sticky stuff off his face. 'You're fucking dead.'

'Oh, please, Graham,' I replied, poking him on the top

190

lip with the muzzle of the pistol. 'No threats. I thought we were all friends here. Ex-colleagues exchanging notes. You know the sort of thing.'

'You're crazy, man,' said Graham. 'Everyone's looking for you for attempted murder and—'

'And you found me,' I interrupted, not really wanting to hear a list of other charges that might be taken into consideration. I didn't have all night. 'Or should I say I found you. And from what I've been hearing, Graham baby, there might be a few charges with your name attached. What do you say to that?'

'I don't know what you're talking about.'

'The angels are listening, Graham. And if you tell porkies you'll never get to heaven. How about conspiracy to rob 4F Security?'

That shut him up.

'Gotcha,' I said.

52

'Bollocks,' he rasped. 'You don't know what you're on about.'

'Pull the other one, Graham, it's got a bell on it. Philip Bell probably.'

'You're full of shit.'

'Is that any way for you to talk?' I said. 'It's you and me from here on in, pal. The Lone Ranger and Tonto. Mel Gibson and Danny Glover. It's like *Lethal Weapon*, *The Next Generation*. And this here is my lethal weapon.' I pushed the snub of the automatic up one of his nostrils. 'And it's fucking loaded, Graham. And no one knows we're here. It's shit or get off the pot time, my old friend. So tell me about that big robbery a while back. And Harry Stonehouse and Tony Lambretta and Uncle Tom Sodding Cobley and all. Because until you do we're joined at the hip, my old son. And I tell you what, it's going to be a whole lot more comfortable for me than it is for you. Take my word. Because my word is my bond.'

He looked at me and sneered. 'Fuck right off,' was all he said.

'OK, Graham, I can see we're going to have to do this the hard way. You still living in that dump in East Dulwich?'

No answer.

''Course you are,' I went on. 'And still on your own, yeah? No woman'll have you, will they? Still. You can't

192

blame them with your personal habits, can you? I think we'll pop round yours and have a cuppa. What do you say?'

The reply was still silence.

I turned round, started the car and drove the short distance to where Graham Jackson had lived as long as I'd known him. 'You might as well tell me,' I said, when I stopped the car outside the small terraced house I remembered from the days when I used to call coppers my mates.

Another blank.

'No,' I said. 'OK. Have it your way.' And I took the automatic and popped Jackson another one on the noggin. Not hard. Just enough to keep him quiet and occupied whilst I checked.

I took the keys out of the ignition and tried the front door with the Chubb key that was on the ring. It worked. I walked down the short corridor and used the Yale that was also on the fob. That worked too. I crept inside, switching on lights as I went. The place was a tip, smelled a bit like a mouse's cage and was empty with no signs of more than one occupant. I checked the living room, single bedroom, K & B, and all was serene. Then I went back for Jackson.

The street was empty and he was moaning gently as I wrestled him out of the car and into the house. 'No noise now, Graham,' I whispered as we went. 'Let's keep this party private.'

I hustled him into the flat and dropped him on the sofa in the living room on top of a pile of newspapers and dirty clothes. 'Cleaning lady not been in this week?' I said. But all I got in reply was a particularly nasty word.

I went into the kitchen, damped down a grubby tea towel and took it back to him. I slapped him round the face with it to wake him up properly, then went through his pockets. Warrant card. Wallet, with a few quid inside, but not enough to even bother nicking it. Cigarettes. Zippo lighter. A few bob in change and a packet of gum. I dropped his stuff on the seat next to him, then perched on the arm of the chair opposite where he was sitting, and said, 'Come on now, Graham. I haven't got all night. Tell me all about it.'

'Fuck off.'

'Graham,' I said feigning weariness, which in fact I felt, 'we're not writing a book here. We don't need to pad out the plot for a few more pages. I want the truth, and I want it within the foreseeable future.'

He shook his head.

I changed the subject then. 'Got any drugs, Graham? It's getting late and I want to be alert.'

Silence.

'If I remember rightly you used to always keep a little stash behind your dear old mum's Bible.'

I stood up, stuck the Browning in my waistband and went to the bookcase. Sure enough, hidden away behind a massive old-fashioned Bible printed in Welsh, was a lacquered box. Inside was some hash and grass, papers and a round black 35mm film canister. 'Holiday snaps, is it?' I asked as I twisted the top off the small container. Inside was a quantity of white powder. I licked up a few grains. 'I thought so,' I said, pouring some of the stuff into the web of my thumb and hoovering it up. 'Good gear, Graham,' I commented as I got a rush. 'Very good.'

I put the canister down, took the gun out again and sat back on the arm of the chair. 'Now let's get serious,' I said.

'They'll miss me at the nick if I don't turn in,' Jackson said after a moment or two.

'You're on lates, aren't you?' I said. 'And this won't take that long. I learned a really good game off a mutual friend of ours the other day. I think we should have a go.'

194

'What game?' He looked a little queasy as he said it, and for the first time I think he realized what a spot he was in.

'It's called Russian Roulette,' I said, put the automatic into one pocket and took the Colt out of the other. I popped out the cylinder, removed the four remaining bullets and showed them to Jackson. 'They're real,' I said. Then I lined them up on the sideboard next to me in a row, took one, dropped it into one of the chambers, closed the gun, held back the hammer and spun the cylinder. Then let the hammer back down.

'You're fucking mad,' said Jackson, the words catching in his throat.

'True,' I said. 'Now some people, Graham, would be most scared if I aimed this at their head. But you – no.' And I pointed the gun at his groin and pulled the trigger.

53

Graham Jackson pissed his pants as the hammer clicked down on an empty chamber. Just like Larry. He threw himself forward, protecting his private parts as I half cocked the gun again and spun the cylinder, then pulled the hammer all the way back. 'Want another go?' I asked.

Jesus, but I was glad the gun hadn't gone off. But then, not half as glad as Jackson was. Count on it.

'You bastard,' he croaked. 'I'll get you for this. You'll go down for ten years by the time I'm finished with you.'

I had to smile. 'No, Graham,' I said. 'Because the way you're going your bollocks will be bolognaise before I'm finished with you. And I'll fucking kill you if I have to. No fingerprints. No witnesses, and this gun is untraceable. Think about it.'

And I pulled the trigger again.

That was when he started to cry.

I flipped out the cylinder and put in a second bullet, closed it, spun it, and pulled back the hammer again. 'Odds are shortening,' I said.

'All right. All right,' he sobbed. 'I'll tell you.'

'That's better,' I said.

'Will you untie me?'

'No chance.'

'Look, this is embarrassing.'

'The more embarrassed you are the better, Graham,' I said, picking up the tea towel and wiping the snot off his face. 'And the sooner you get all this off your chest the quicker you can get a pair of clean strides on.'

I pushed him upright and pulled the chair I was sitting on closer. 'Now come on, son,' I said. 'Tell me all.'

'Philip Bell was after Stonehouse from the day the robbery went down,' he explained. 'He knew that Stonehouse had used the information from 4F to set up the blag. He just knew. You know what I mean?'

I nodded. Sure I knew. Call it hunch or intuition or whatever you want. Good coppers always have it. Bad coppers don't even know it exists. They call it luck. Bollocks to luck, I say. You make your own luck in this life.

'We were mates,' Graham went on. 'I wasn't working on the case officially, but me and Phil would meet up for a drink and talk about it. Know what I mean?'

'Yeah,' I said. 'I know exactly what you mean.'

'Then one night Philip says. "What would you do if we got hold of that money and no one knew?" Me. I says keep it, and that was that really. After that we worked together on breaking Harry Stonehouse down.'

'And you succeeded.'

'In the end. We got him to grass on the players that he knew about.'

'But not the bosses. The planners.'

'Not the real boss.'

'Tony Lambretta.'

'That's the one. Bastard.'

'But you got the money out of Harry.'

'Yeah. We got the money. Or most of it.'

'How much?'

'About fifteen million in cash. The rest had already been sorted out between them.'

'And where is it now?'

197

He hesitated, and I could see conflicting emotions racing across his face.

'Graham,' I said, hefting the pistol.

'All right, all right. It's in a container at a storage place in Croydon. Purley Way. Know it?'

'I know it. What's the deal there?'

'It's open twenty-four hours. It's got security. The usual.'

'Cheers, Graham. That wasn't all that hard, was it?'

'What are you going to do now?' he asked.

'Take a share, Graham. That's all,' I lied. 'Just a share for me and Robber and Nancy Stonehouse.'

'That fucking bike.'

'You been there too, Graham?' I said. 'How nice. That makes all of us, doesn't it?'

'You're not going to take it all?'

I shook my head. 'But tell me, Graham,' I said. 'How come Harry ended up like he did?'

'Don't ask me. He was stuck into a witness protection scheme. New identity, the lot. He ended up down in Bristol. He had a decent place, money. Everything. Then the silly fucker blew it somehow and ended up dead.'

'Was he due a cut of the profits you and Bell were going to share?'

''Course he was. Philip was going to take an early retirement next year. Start up his own security firm which he could use to launder the dough. Then he was going to offer me a job and I'd leave the force.'

'That's nice,' I said. 'A security firm run on bent money. Talk about setting thieves to catch thieves. Or murderers as it turns out.'

'You don't think we done for Harry, do you?' said Jackson, so full of injured innocence it almost made me puke.

198

'No, I don't as a matter of fact, Graham. I know exactly who done for Harry and who dumped him all over London town.'

'Lambretta,' said Jackson.

'It doesn't take a genius to work it out. The only thing I want to know is who sold Harry out to him. Now that could've been you. Or Philip. Or both of you.'

54

'Why should we bother?' he said. 'Everything was sweet. Why spoil it?'

'How the fuck should I know? Why do people like you do anything? Maybe one of you just fancied a bigger share. But that's irrelevant. Let me tell you what's going to happen now.'

'What?'

'You say you've got access to the storage place where the money is twenty-four hours.'

'Yeah.'

'But not much goes on at night?'

'Not a lot.'

'Right, then,' I said. 'Tonight.' I looked at my watch. It was nearly half-three. 'In exactly twenty-four hours' time, three-thirty tomorrow morning, you, me and Philip Bell are going to meet down in Purley. We go in. I take my share and leave. Simple as that.'

I could see his devious little mind working behind his blue eyes.

'But before you get any bright ideas, I'm going to make sure enough people know about the meet, so that if anything happens to me – Like f'r'instance I just vanish into thin air – someone will come looking. Get me?'

'But—'

'No buts,' I interrupted. 'The people I tell will have no idea what's really happening. Just some names and a place.

But I will make sure that if I don't show up again, full details of what's been happening will end up on the Commissioner's desk. Do I make myself clear?'

Jackson nodded.

'It makes sense, Graham. I'm not greedy. I just want something to make the last few days worthwhile. You'll have plenty left to start up your security firm, or retire to Montserrat if that's your pleasure. I ain't gonna grass you up. It wouldn't make sense. So get hold of Bell and I'll see you down the storage place tomorrow morning.'

I could still see his evil little mind working.

'And Graham,' I said.

'What?'

'Don't even think about moving the gear and being here all safely tucked up in bed while I'm standing outside the storage place like a lemon. Because I'll come and find you. That's a promise. And I bet you've read everything there is to read about me. You know I mean it, don't you?'

He nodded.

'Because I'm like a bad dream to you, Graham. See, I don't give a flying fuck about anything these days. Not a thing.'

And I calmly put the Colt against my temple and pulled the trigger. Graham Jackson jumped when the hammer went down on another empty chamber, but I didn't. And I knew then that I was beyond hope or help or anything like that.

'All right,' he said after a moment's thought. 'But if you try—'

'Save it, Graham,' I said. 'You're in no position to make threats.'

Not that I was particularly, but then I had an idea. I

walked back over to the sofa and picked up his warrant. 'I'm going to borrow this,' I said.

'No.'

'Don't worry, son, you can have it back. I just need it for something. I won't drop you in it. Right, I'm off now.' I checked the wire that bound his wrists and loosened it a touch. 'You'll be out of that in ten minutes. Just time for me to make myself scarce. Don't forget our meeting, will you? I'd hate to turn up and find no one there. Or alternatively a couple of van loads of woodentops. Because either way you and Bell will be in deep shit.'

He nodded again, and I left, taking the two other .38 Special bullets with me. I remembered that there was a mini-cab office a couple of streets away, but as I reached the main road one of those things happened that makes living in London worthwhile. From up the deserted street I saw a lone black cab with its FOR HIRE sign lit. I flagged it down and the driver dropped me off in Maida Vale. It was light by then, and I walked the last of the way to Diane's flat where I found her fast asleep in bed. And all the way I could hear the echo of that hammer coming down on air, and I can still hear it to this day.

55

I managed to grab a couple of hours' kip next to Diane before she woke me getting ready for her first day back at work. 'What were you up to all night?' she asked.

'Business,' I said.

'Monkey business, I reckon. What are you doing today?'

'More business,' I replied sleepily. 'Don't know when I'll see you.' Or if I ever would again. I was going to play all ends against the middle and it was going to be extremely dangerous. But I didn't care. In fact I was looking forward to it.

Diane gave me a cup of coffee in bed and a brief kiss. 'See you later,' she said.

'God willing,' I replied to her back as she left the room. I felt a pang of something as she left, but I wasn't sure what. Indigestion, maybe.

I leant back against the pillow and lit a cigarette. I needed a plan to get all the main players together in – what? I checked my watch – nineteen and a half hours. I grinned, dropped the butt into my cup and headed for the bathroom.

When I was shaved, washed and dressed I called Nancy. 'I'm going to need you and your car today,' I said. 'And it's going to be a late one.'

'Have you found something?'

'Something,' I replied. 'Meet me outside Maida Vale tube at ten.'

'I'll be there.'

'Good,' I said and broke the connection.

Next up was Tony Lambretta. I called the number that Harry Stonehouse had written in his address book on my mobile.

A male voice answered the phone after three rings. I wondered if it was the John Duncan I'd kicked in the head. 'Mr Lambretta,' I said.

'Who wants him?'

'Nick Sharman.'

There was a pause. 'You've got some fucking nerve phoning here.'

It was. 'How's the head?' I asked.

'You bastard. Be careful, Sharman. One day you'll turn round and I'll be there.'

'What? Looking for your wallet? I bought me and the bird a nice meal on your Access. Cheers. Now I'd love to chat but time's a-wasting. Get me Lambretta. Tell him it's something to his advantage.'

The phone went down with a bang and I was left listening to air for a long three minutes. Not even any muzak for company. Eventually I heard the receiver being picked up. 'What?' barked a deep voice.

'Mr Lambretta. Nick Sharman here.'

'I know who it is. What do you want?'

'I've found the money.'

'Bollocks you have.'

'Believe me. It wasn't difficult. Not with my contacts.'

'Where is it?'

'Hold on. Not so fast. I want my share, don't I?'

'Don't worry, I'll sort ya.'

Sure, I thought. Into a few black garbage bags if I'm lucky. 'You'll need a few mates,' I said. 'There might be some rough stuff.'

'I've got plenty.'

'I'm sure. Get them ready for tonight.'

'What time?'

'Three-thirty. I'll let you know the details later. You got a mobile number?'

''Course.' He reeled off ten digits and I scribbled them down on a piece of paper.

'I'll talk to you later,' I said. 'With the full SP.'

'This better not be a wind-up.'

'It ain't. Trust me. We'll talk soon. And I don't want any trouble with Duncan. Keep him on a short leash.'

'I will.'

'Good,' I said and cut her off.

That'd give him something to think about.

56

Nancy was waiting for me when I got to the tube station. 'What's happening?' she asked.

'You'll find out,' I replied. 'In the fullness of time.'

'So where are we going?'

'Dalston. The General Hospital.'

'Why?'

'You'll find out. In the fullness of time.'

'Have I offended you in some way, Nick?' she asked.

'You'll find out. In the fullness of time. Now drive. And keep to the speed limit. I'm armed, and I don't need a pull.'

She did as she was told, even though she kept asking questions all the way that I fended off as well as I could, and after a couple of false starts we ended up in the parking lot at Dalston General. 'You wait here,' I said. 'Don't leave. I don't know how long I'll be. I've got to see a man about a dog. I'll meet you back here as soon as I can.'

'OK,' she said. 'Don't worry. I'll be here.'

'Good,' I said, quit the car and headed for the back entrance.

I found a hospital register on the wall by the lift. Intensive Care was on the fifth floor and I headed upwards. I found an orderly who, after I showed him Jackson's warrant, covering as much of his photo as I could with my finger, checked his clipboard and told me that Robber had been transferred down to a private room on the third floor. That was a good sign, and I used the emergency stairs to go down. There was a redheaded sister sitting on the desk by the door. I brought out Jackson's brief again and flashed it at her, using the old finger trick again. 'Police,' I said. 'DS Jackson from Denmark Hill, looking for Jack Robber.'

She smiled at me most engagingly. 'You're a long way from home,' she said in a soft Irish accent. I must confess I was smitten.

'Old friend,' I said. 'You know he used to be on the force.'

'Word gets around. He's in three one seven.'

'How is he?' I asked.

'Being a nuisance. Which I imagine means he's getting better.'

I kept a straight face. 'Any of my colleagues about?' I asked.

'No. Not any more. They were with him all the time at first, I believe . . .'

'Manpower,' I said. 'Overtime. You know how it is.'

'It's the same everywhere,' she said. 'I could tell you some stories.'

Anytime, I thought. 'Specially in private, with her in her nurse's uniform and black stockings, but I had other fish to fry. 'I bet,' I said. 'Can I go straight in?'

'Yes. But he might shout at you.'

'I think I can deal with it,' I said, smiled, winked just in case we ever met again, and headed in the direction in which she pointed me.

I tapped on the door of room three one seven and opened it. The shades were drawn and it was cool and dim inside with only the muted sound of daytime TV to disturb the peace. I walked over to the bed which contained a figure holding up that day's *Express* in front of his face, and I said, 'Morning, Jack. How's your bad luck?'

The paper went down and he looked at me. 'Well now,' he said. 'Look who's here.'

'They think I'm Graham Jackson,' I explained. 'Don't disillusion them.'

'I won't ask why,' he said. 'But I assume you've been busy in my absence.'

'Yes,' I replied. 'How are you?'

'Thanks for asking. I'll survive.'

'It was close, I think,' I said.

'Did you call the ambulance?'

I nodded.

'Then shot shit out of the police car.'

Another nod.

He laughed out loud. 'Christ, I wish I'd been there.'

'You were.'

'So I believe. Thanks, by the way. You saved my life by all accounts.'

I was relieved he took it like that.

'Have you told the coppers what really happened that night?' I asked him. 'They think I shot you. You know that?'

'Not you. Someone else.'

'Jack, I was there. The coppers and paramedics saw me.'

'Not well enough for ID. You were covered in blood, and it was dark, remember. I had an old mate at Dalston, a DS, come in, and he told me all. The two uniforms and the ambulance crew couldn't say for sure who it was, and I assured him you were nowhere near.'

'But I've done a runner.'

'On holiday I said. Welsh Wales, camping. No phones, no papers. A complete break.'

'And they believed that shit?'

'No. But what could they do about it?'

208

'What about the car?'

'What car?'

'The Audi I borrowed that the Bill found covered in blood in Maida Vale. They gave my mate a good spin about that.'

'Coincidence. No prints. You always wore those stupid gloves.'

'You didn't.'

'But I was careful. I always am. Anyway, how often do fingerprints figure in a case outside Inspector sodding Wexford stories?'

That's the truth. 'Did you tell them who really shot you?' I asked.

He shook his head. 'No. Just some geezers. An old score maybe. I made some enemies.'

'Were you still thinking about the money?'

'Maybe. I dunno. But we can forget about that now.'

'No, Jack,' I said. 'I've got a couple of scores to settle myself.'

'If you just kept your head down, you'd be all right, and this would all blow over.'

'I'm tall, with a big head, Jack,' I replied. 'I find it very difficult to keep it down.' Then I changed the subject. 'Did your widow woman tell you I called?' I asked.

It was his turn to give me a nod.

'And Diane tried a couple of times. Pretended she was your niece. Got a lot of old hassle.'

'I heard about that too. My sister let it out she had no children. Good move.'

'I wondered.'

'Bloody woman. She just won't leave well enough alone. Call box. Right?'

A third nod from me.

209

'Good thinking. At least they couldn't trace.'

'How long before you're out of here?' I asked.

He shrugged. 'God knows.'

'But you're better now. Out of danger.'

'Look at me. What do *you* think? No. Don't answer. When you're around everyone's in danger.'

'Sorry,' I said. 'But I've been worried.'

'Really?'

'Yeah. I was getting used to you being around.'

'Well you can stop all that old bollocks for a start. You'll have me in sodding tears. If you're determined to keep putting your nose where it's not wanted, you'd better tell me what's been happening.'

I told him. Everything, from the moment he'd been shot until the present.

He listened without interrupting, then said, 'Good work. But you're playing with fire trying to handle this all on your own.'

'Piece of cake,' I said, with more confidence than I felt. 'And tonight we're all going to meet at the storage place.'

'All?'

'The lot. Cops, bikers, blaggers, Nancy and me.'

'Where do the bikers come in?'

'You'll see.'

'And then? When you're all together, what happens?'

'And then, Jack, I reckon there's going to be a whole load of trouble.'

57

I looked at my watch. It was already past noon and I had lots more to do before I was finished. 'I'm going,' I said. 'You might hear about it on the news.'

'And you might disappear, and I'll read about you being found in black sacks in a few weeks like Harry was.'

That was exactly what I was scared of.

But, 'Just keep the TV on,' was all I said, and I shook his hand when he assured me it wasn't going to give him any grief in his injured shoulder, and I left. On the way out I waved to the sister and she waved back. Maybe it would be my lucky day after all.

Nancy was waiting where I'd left her. 'Everything OK?' she asked.

'Just fine.'

'Nick, tell me.'

'OK,' I said after a moment. 'I know where the money is and we're going to get it tonight.'

She looked at me in astonishment. 'You've found it?'

'That's my job,' I said. 'There's many a slip, though. We've got to be careful.'

'Who had it?'

'A couple of your old boyfriends. Philip Bell and Graham Jackson.'

At least she had the good grace to blush.

'Those bastards,' she said. 'I never knew.'

'You can't trust anyone these days,' I said as dryly as I could.

'Where did they get it?' she asked, ignoring my tone, or more probably not even hearing it.

'Harry gave it to them.'

'*What?*'

'It's true. He sold out the gang to get protection, then let our friends in on where the money was hidden. They liberated it, and stashed it away. If Harry had stayed put where he was, he'd've got a share. But he just couldn't leave you alone, could he?'

'It wasn't my fault.'

'No?'

'No. He never told me where the money was. He said he'd never seen it.'

'Whatever. Anyway, tonight we go and get it.'

'Is it safe?'

'I'm trying my best to make sure. I need to go to Peckham.'

'Why?'

'Enough already. I've told you everything you need to know for now. Trust me.'

She gave me an old-fashioned look and started the car.

58

Nervous Norbert Green wasn't in the Angel of Mercy, but his mate the barman was. As soon as he saw me he decided he had business in the back. I waited patiently until the punters started getting a bit stroppy at the lack of service and he was called back by the landlady who'd served me. I watched as he pulled their pints, and he kept looking at me out of the corner of his eye until he passed close by and I said, 'Norbert been in?'

'I don't know any Norbert,' he said.

I grabbed him by his skinny tie and pulled him half-way over the jump. 'Don't fuck about, son,' I whispered into his ear. 'Unless you fancy choking to death.'

He was going very red in the face but no one interfered. I suspected that such a show was pretty regular in that neck of the woods if you'll excuse the pun, but nevertheless I eased off the pressure and he pulled back, coughing and spluttering. 'Too many fags, son,' I said. 'Bad for the wind.'

'Norbert's not been in,' he said eventually. 'Why don't you leave him alone? Didn't you get him into enough trouble the last time?'

'And now I'm here to get him out of trouble,' I said. 'Got an address?'

'You think I'd give it to you?'

'Yeah,' I said. 'Otherwise I'm going to beat you to a sodding pulp.'

He gave me the address then. A men's hostel just up the

road. 'Cheers,' I said as I left. 'If you see him before I do, be sure to tell him I'm looking, will you?'

I went back to where I'd left Nancy in the car and we drove to the address the barman had given me. After I dropped him a score, the caretaker, or whatever they called him – probably the *concierge* in these poncy times – told me that Norbert had gone out early as he usually did. 'Probably up the hospital,' he said.

Oops, I thought.

I got Nancy to drive back into Peckham and she parked up the car and I left her in a café drinking coffee and reading the local paper as I started scoping the pubs. And there's a hell of a lot of pubs in Peckham.

I tried the Pit Pony, the Sacred Heart, the Golden Fleece, the Frog In Petticoats and what seemed like two dozen more in and around the main drag. No sign of Norbert. Then I started on the pubs in the side streets. It was well past three before I went into the darkest, seediest boozer yet. A beer shop at the end of a cul-de-sac called the Little Red Engine. And there was Norbert sitting in the corner in front of a pint and a brimming ashtray.

As soon as he saw me he tried to head towards the back exit, but I caught him easy, threw him back in his seat and ordered a couple of large scotches.

He looked like he needed one. His head was bandaged, and from what I could see of the wound that seemed to cover one whole half of his head, it appeared that someone had taken a chain-saw to his face.

'Let me guess,' I said.

'Leave me alone,' he said.

I pushed the gold watch in front of him and he downed it in one, so I ordered another. 'Had an accident, Norbert?' I asked.

'It was that fucking Larry,' he said. 'I thought you weren't going to mention my name.'

'Sorry about that,' I said. 'It just slipped out.'

'And look at me now.'

'Want to get back in his good books?' I asked.

'I don't want nothing more to do with him.'

'Sorry, mate, but I insist.'

He slumped back in his seat. 'What do you want?' he almost sobbed.

'Remember you told me he was always wanting to know when a big coke deal was going down so that him and his gang could hijack it?'

Norbert just nodded, the skin on the uninjured side of his face white against the lividity of the wound.

'Right,' I said. 'You got a number for him?'

He started to shake his head, but I think it hurt him too much, and with tears in his eyes he said, 'I've got his portable.'

I took out my mobile phone and wrote the address of the storage place on the back of a beer mat. 'Give him a bell, Norbert,' I said. 'Tell him there's a big, no, a *massive* deal going down there tomorrow morning at three-thirty precisely. That'll get you back on his good side.'

'Is there?'

'Well something's going down, and I want him and his boys there.'

'Jesus, I'll get killed,' said Norbert.

'But later, Norbert,' I said. 'Or maybe never if it all works out. Of course the alternative is for me to kill you now.' And I showed him the butt of the Browning.

59

Nervous Norbert made the call just like I told him to, even though it took him several tries to get through, his fingers were trembling so much. Eventually he made the connection and got Crazy Larry on the line. He sounded sincere enough as he laid out the story, and only a couple of times did he have to insist that he was telling the truth. By the time he turned off the phone his whole body was shaking and the good side of his face was slick with perspiration.

'Good work, Norbert,' I said, counting out a oner from my dwindling cash supply. 'I'd make yourself scarce if I were you. And don't think about calling Larry back. It'd be bad for your health. At least right now you've got one good eye.'

And with that I left, and went back to find Nancy.

She was still sitting where I'd left her. 'You took your time,' she said. 'I was about to give up, and I'm just about drowning in bad coffee.'

'He was hard to find,' I said. 'But I got him in the end.'

'Who the hell is he, anyway?' she asked.

'Just a mate,' I said.

'What now, then?' she asked as we left the café.

'Now we go down to Croydon. I don't trust Bell and Jackson further than I can throw them. I just want to keep an eye on the place until rendezvous time.'

'And when's that?' she asked.

'Three-thirty tomorrow morning.'

'But that's hours yet,' she protested.

'Then you'd better go to the loo now and get rid of some of that coffee,' I said.

60

On the way from Peckham to Croydon I made a couple of calls. First of all I got Graham Jackson on the line at Denmark Hill. 'Everything Mellow-D Graham?' I asked when he picked up the phone.

'Man, but you're walking a thin line,' he replied.

'What? Between love and hate?' I asked.

He didn't get the allegory. Not a big sixties soul fan our Graham, I surmised.

'What the fuck you on about?' was all he said.

'Forget it,' I replied. 'We still on for tonight?'

'Yeah.'

'You spoken to Brother Bell?'

'Yeah.'

'Happy man, is he?'

'Don't take the piss, son, or it'll be the worse for you.'

'Can you hear my teeth chattering, Gray?'

'Don't get over-confident.'

'With mugs like you around how could I be anything else? See you later, pal.'

And I cut him off. Then I tried Fulham nick. Bell was at his desk. 'You think you're a clever bastard, don't you, Sharman?' he said when I told him who it was.

'Just trying to turn a shilling, Phil,' I replied.

'My shilling.'

'But hardly honest, Phil. That's the thing. Now you

218

haven't gone all clever on me and moved anything, have you?'

I figured that fifteen million in notes was going to be hard to find a home for at such short notice. You could hardly chuck it into the hatchback and drive it round until you found a friendly bank or building society.

'No.'

'Then it's fair shares all round. Come on, Philip, there's plenty for everyone.'

'If you say so.'

And then I knew he planned to kill me.

Chance would be a fine thing, I thought, and I touched the pistol in my pocket for good luck.

'I'm not greedy, Philip. I promise.'

In fact I really didn't want any of it.

'You'd better not be.'

These geezers loved to make threats.

'It's the truth. All I want is a bit of a result for me, Robber and Nancy, and everything will be copacetic.'

'I believe you.'

'Good. Now can we get into this place OK?'

'You can with my say-so. There's an old boy in the gatehouse at night. I'll tell him I'm expecting you.'

'Don't use my name,' I said.

'I'm not stupid,' he replied. 'And don't use mine. Down there I'm known as Mr Bridger. Graham is Mr Talbot. Got it?'

'Got it.'

'I'll tell the security bloke your name's Ford.'

'Ford.'

'Like the car.'

'Whatever you say. So I'll see you later.'

'We'll be there.'

219

'I'm counting on you.'

And then I cut him off too. And if he believed that I believed what he said, then he must've thought I'd believe anything.

61

We got to the Purley Way about five and cruised down until I saw the storage firm on our right. Bang opposite was a side street with a pub on the corner. 'Pull in there,' I said. 'Let's get a drink.'

Nancy parked up and we went into the boozer, which was small and old-fashioned, but had a table by the window where you could see the building across the street. I bought a couple of drinks and we sat. 'What now?' she said.

'We wait.'

'Until three-thirty tomorrow morning?'

'That's the plan, Nancy,' I said, looking over at the high razor-wire-topped fence that surrounded the place, interrupted only by a wooden barrier that was operated from inside a small glass gatehouse. There was a sign on the fence that said: CUSTOMER PARKING AT REAR.

'On second thoughts,' I said, 'perhaps we should go in.'

'When?'

'Now. Take a shufti. Pretend we need to rent some space.'

'Both of us?'

'Sure. It looks better if there's a woman there, but let me do the talking.'

'You've got it all worked out, haven't you, Nick?'

'I try.'

But all the same I wondered what would happen if Bell and Jackson just called my bluff and didn't turn up at the designated time. I'd look pretty stupid sitting in Croydon with my thumb up my arse while they were in some all-night drinker laughing their socks off.

'At least it'll pass some time,' said Nancy.

'You're right. Come on.'

We drank up and returned to the car. Nancy did a U-turn and we went back on to Purley Way, up to the roundabout and back, and turned into the entrance of Firmin's Security Inc. There was a security bloke inside the gatehouse, but all he did was press a button and the barrier lifted.

Nancy drove through and followed the signs that led to the parking area. Once there we left the car again and went through a glass door marked RECEPTION.

Behind a big desk was a bimbo in a blue uniform with hair like candy floss and big blue eyes made even bigger with the same shade of mascara that Margaret Thatcher used to wear. The name tag on her left breast read Ursula. I wondered what the other one was called.

'Good afternoon, sir, madam,' she said. 'Can I be of any assistance?'

'I hope so,' I said. 'My wife and I are going abroad for a while and want to store some of our stuff, and we were wondering what the form was.'

'Well,' she said, smiling, 'our boast is that we can store anything from a matchbox to a jumbo jet, and our rates are highly competitive.'

'Do you get a lot of call to store jumbo jets?' I asked.

She smiled again. 'No. But we could if pressed. What sort of volume are we talking about here?'

'The contents of a small house. It's difficult...' I hesitated.

'Well, Mr...?' said Ursula.

222

'Norris. Stephen Norris,' I said.

'Mr Norris. What we'd do then is send round one of our assessors. He or she would work out the unit space, then we'd bring round one of our containers, pack up your stuff for you in boxes, load it on board, bring it back here, remove the container from the lorry and store it in the warehouse. You have twenty-four-hour-a-day access, your own key or keys to the container, fully comprehensive insurance, and we charge by the month or part thereof.'

'And it's secure.'

'We like to think so. Would you care to inspect our facilities?'

That's just what I'd hoped she'd suggest.

'Please,' I said.

'One moment.' She picked up a phone and dialled. After a second, she said, 'Michael. Would you come through, please.'

She put down the phone and said to me, 'He'll be right with you. When would you want to store your possessions?'

'In about a month's time,' I replied.

'No problem.'

We were interrupted when a man came through the door behind her. He too wore a blue uniform, but as far as I could make out no mascara. His name tag said Michael.

'Michael,' said Ursula. 'This is Mr and Mrs Norris. They're thinking of storing their household contents with us for a while. They'd like a quick tour.'

'No problem,' said the man to her. Then to us, 'If you'll just step this way.'

'And on your way out if I may take some details,' said Ursula.

'Of course,' I said, and Nancy and I followed Michael through the door he'd used to come in.

That led into a carpeted foyer with more glass doors on both sides and a plain wooden one to the front of us. 'To your left and right,' said Michael, 'are the entrances to our safety deposit box vaults. But it sounds like you'll be needing a container. Is that right?'

I nodded, and he pushed the plain door that led into the warehouse proper. It was big inside, huge, in fact, and probably could take a 747 at a pinch. The place was full of oblong metal boxes ranging in size from something that would fit on the back of a pick-up truck to ones that would need an articulated lorry to carry them. They were neatly stacked up, one on top of each other, half a dozen or more deep as far as the eye could see, except where two huge doors that looked out on to the main road were rolled up into the ceiling to allow lorries to enter to load and unload.

'How do you get to the top ones?' I asked.

Michael pointed upwards. The whole roof was lined with cranes on gantries. 'Easy,' he said. 'We can have any container on the floor within three minutes.'

'Very efficient,' I said.

'We think so. Is there anything else you'd like to see?'

'No. Except what happens if we need something in the middle of the night?'

'No problem. We only have a skeleton staff between seven p.m. and seven a.m., but everything here is so automated that one man could run the whole place. You just turn up any time, twenty-four hours a day, three hundred and sixty-five days a year, and you can get to your property. However, if you should want to move a container out during the night or on public holidays we do ask for at least twenty-four hours' notice.'

'Fair enough,' I said.

He led us back to the reception area where I gave Ursula

224

a fake address and telephone number which she wrote down on a booking form.

'We'll let you know within a few days,' I said.

'That'll be fine,' she replied, giving me a glossy brochure and price list. 'I hope we can facilitate you here.'

'I'm sure you can,' I said, smiled, took Nancy's arm, went back to the car and she drove us out on to the Purley Way again.

62

'Where to?' she asked.

'Back to the boozer,' I replied. 'I fancy a real drink and something to eat.'

She parked the car round the back of the pub and we went in and I ordered more drinks. As the evening wore on I saw Ursula, Michael and the rest of the day shift come out of Firmin's and drive or walk off, and the night people go inside. There weren't many, about four as far as I could make out. A couple of security men we'd seen over there earlier came over for a drink but didn't pay us any attention. According to a blackboard mounted on the wall, there was a choice of delicious bar snacks available behind the counter, and Nancy and I sampled a couple. They tasted like cardboard. Delicious bar cardboard, but cardboard nevertheless.

Around ten I went out to the gents, checked that it was empty and called Lambretta from my mobile on his land line. He answered himself. 'Are you screwin' around?' was the first thing he said.

'What me? No chance, Tone. Just taking care of business.'

'So where's this money?'

'Don't worry. It's safe. Everything's arranged for tomorrow morning.'

'Where are you?'

'In a pub.'

'Jesus.'

'Don't worry, son, I won't let you down. I'll call after closing time. That'll give you plenty of time to get where you're going. Just be ready.'

'I've been ready all sodding day.'

'I've been ready all my sodding life,' I replied and shut him down.

I went back to Nancy and she'd ordered another round. Good job, I thought as the liquor burned its way down to my belly. Tonight I'm going to need all the courage I can find.

They slung us out around eleven-thirty and we went back to the car and moved it round so that we could see the entrance to the storage facility, but deep in the shadows so as not to be obvious. All was quiet, but I figured that wouldn't last long. We'd bought cigarettes and rolled the windows down and sat there as the big harvest moon moved round the sky and three-thirty got closer.

63

I got out of the car at ten to one on the pretext of stretching my legs and called Lambretta again. 'Show time,' I said and told him the full details of time and place. 'And don't go steaming in like loonies. Give us a chance to get to the cash. Step softly, Tone. This is the one chance we get. There's only four staff on at night. Three in the main building, one in the gatehouse out front. So you don't need to be too heavy-handed. Be cool.'

'I'll do what needs to be done,' was his terse reply.

'I'm counting on it,' I said, and broke the connection.

The last two hours of our wait crept by painfully slowly. Nancy and I had exhausted all topics of conversation, the radio stations seemed to be broadcasting nothing but citizens whingeing on talk shows, and the seats in her car were thin and uncomfortable. I passed the time mentally ticking off all the ways my plan, if you could justify it by calling it a plan, could go wrong. More ways than it could go right to be honest. But that was the way things were usually with my plans – and why change the habits of a lifetime?

But finally the hands on my watch crept past three and I rubbed the weariness out of my eyes and started to look with more interest at the cars that sped down the Purley Way.

I noticed two at least that slowed as they passed the front gate, then turned at the lights without indicating. Lambretta, I figured, and I hoped he and his people had the sense not to steam in with guns blazing.

Then, at three-thirty precisely, a dark saloon pulled into the entrance of Firmin's and the gate guard came out, bent to speak to the driver, made a note on the clipboard he carried, returned to the gatehouse and raised the barrier.

'Is that them?' asked Nancy.

'There's only one way to find out,' I said. 'Leave the car here.'

We got out of the motor and crossed the wide expanse of sodium-light-splashed, deserted main road, and went up to the gatehouse ourselves.

The guard gave us a cross-eyed look as we approached his cage, but I smiled my most charming smile and said, 'We're expected. My name's Ford. We're due to meet a Mr Bridger at three-thirty. Was that him?'

'That's right, sir,' said the guard. 'He told me he was expecting you. Don't you have a car?'

'We got a lift,' I replied. 'Mr Bridger will drop us off later.'

'Just go up to the main entrance,' said the guard. 'There'll be someone to let you in there. Go to the big glass doors.'

'Cheers,' I said, and together Nancy and I walked up the drive to the hulk of the warehouse that loomed in front of us, brightly lit by spotlights set in the ground in front of it.

64

The main entrance was at the front of the building and there was another uniformed guard waiting just inside. That afternoon of course we'd gone into the back from the car park, and as the man in the blue uniform unlocked the doors and let us in I tried to get my bearings.

There was a staircase running up from the centre of the foyer with a door on either side. The one on the left was marked RECEPTION, the one on the right VAULTS, so I assumed that if we went through the left-hand door we would come into the other foyer we'd passed through earlier with Michael, and that in its turn would take us into the main warehouse.

'We're looking for Mr Bridger,' I said to the second guard. 'Name's Ford.'

'He's just arrived, sir,' replied the man. 'He's inside the main storage area.'

I'd been right about the geography of the place, and the guard led us through to the warehouse where Bell and Jackson were waiting.

'Hello, Mr Bridger, Mr Talbot,' I said. 'How good of you to come at such short notice.'

The guard gave me a queer look and said, 'Will that be all?' to Bell.

'Fine,' replied Bell, and after the guard had gone through the door back to the foyer, he said to me with a look at Nancy that was usually reserved for shit on the bottom of your best brogues, 'What's the whore doing here?'

'Nice mouth you have there,' I replied. 'Just leave it. She's got a right to be here.'

'I don't want her around.'

'You've got no choice. I say what's happening, not you.'

'You fucker,' said Jackson.

I gave him a similar look to the one Bell had given Nancy. 'Yeah, Graham, you've said that before for all the good it did you. What's happening here exactly?'

'There's a bloke going to work the crane,' Bell said. 'Our stuff's on top of that pile over there.' He pointed with his right hand in no particular direction.

'Then?'

'Then we open it up, go inside out of the way, and you get what you came for.'

'Cheers,' I said, and suddenly all sorts of pulleys and chains burst into life above me. I looked around and saw a glass-fronted control room I hadn't noticed before in one corner of the warehouse. Behind the glass sat a guy in a light blue shirt who manoeuvred one of the large containers off the top of its pile and set it down neatly on the concrete floor a dozen yards from where we were standing.

'That's it?' I asked as the geezer came out of the control room and clambered down a metal ladder attached to the wall.

'That's it,' said Bell, who nodded at the guy as he walked past us, then produced a gold-coloured mortise key from his pocket, Jackson took a similar one from his.

'Shit,' I said. 'Who would've believed all that money was right here all the time?'

'Want to take a look?' said Bell with a shit-eating grin.

Come into my parlour, I thought, as I nodded my head and we walked together over to the container, and wondered if Lambretta and his people had got lost on the way.

231

65

Graham Jackson joined us at the door of the container, inserted his key into one of the two locks and twisted it. Philip Bell did the same to the other, pulled down on the iron bar that secured the door and swung it open on its creaking hinges.

Bell reached inside and switched on what must have been a battery-powered light that sat in the ceiling behind a mesh screen. The bulb was dim, but bright enough to see that the interior of the container was waist deep in grey canvas bags marked with the 4F Security logo and all fastened at the necks with wire. 'Eldorado,' said Bell.

All three of us stepped inside the door and I picked up one of the bags. It was heavy and rustled with paper inside. Wodges of paper. Cash.

'How much in each bag?' I asked.

'Depends,' said Bell. 'This is dead money, don't forget.'

'It's about to come to life,' I replied. 'Or at least some of it is. We'll put what we need into your car and transfer it to ours somewhere quiet.'

'I want my sodding brief back,' said Graham Jackson.

'Don't worry, son,' I said. 'As soon as we've got our dough you'll get it.'

We stepped back out into the warehouse and Nancy was waiting with a gun in her hand. A big gun. A Smith & Wesson .357 Magnum Combat model that looked even bigger in her tiny hands. 'Harry's,' she said by way of explanation. She must have had it in the huge bag she'd been carrying all day. And I didn't look. What a schmuck. 'And I know how to use it. He taught me. So don't get any big ideas about the little woman being afraid of muzzle flash.'

'Stand and deliver,' I said. 'Nancy. What the fuck are you playing at?'

'Not playing,' she replied. 'Being deadly serious.'

'For fuck's sake, Nancy, you're going to spoil everything,' I said almost pleadingly. You'd've pleaded too if you'd been looking down into the big black hole that was the muzzle of the gun.

'Shut up, Nick,' she said. 'And get the guns you're carrying out and on to the floor.'

I did as she told me, placing the Colt and the Browning carefully on the ground in front of me.

'You armed, boys?' she said to Jackson and Bell.

'Course they're armed, I thought. How naïve.

'Find out,' said Bell.

Nancy cocked the S&W and moved the barrel up and down his torso. 'I don't need to find out, lover,' she said. 'I just shoot your balls off. I know what means the most to you.'

Just like I'd done to Graham Jackson at his flat. Funny how all coppers were so fond of their bollocks. It must go with the job.

'OK, OK,' said Bell. 'Graham. Come on.'

They both reached under their jackets. 'Slowly,' said Nancy. 'No tricks.'

'Was this your idea?' said Bell to me after his and Jackson's police issue short-barrelled Webley .38 revolvers were on the floor too.

233

'Are you kidding?' I said back. 'Does it look like my soddin' idea? All I want is a quiet life.'

And on cue, the huge metal doors to the warehouse began to roll up into the ceiling.

66

'What the fuck?' said Bell, turning towards the doors, and all our eyes followed his. Slowly and relentlessly the doors rolled up on their pulleys, and the gatehouse guard was shoved forward and sprawled on the floor in front of us. Behind his prone figure, silhouetted against the lights that shone up against the building outside were half a dozen figures all armed with an assortment of semi-automatic pistols and shotguns. And behind them, its engine running, stood a huge tractor truck with an empty low-loader attached. All the better to carry away the container of cash, I thought.

By sheer reflex Nancy fired the magnum she was holding and the bullet shot sparks off the ground and ricocheted against the metal-clad walls. The figures outside dropped to the ground and returned fire and I felt a tug at my left sleeve and my arm went numb. That was when I took my chance, ducked, snatched up the Browning with thirteen full metal brass-jacketed shells nestling in its magazine like little babies waiting to be born and rip the meat from the bones of anyone who got in their way, and fled into the maze of stacked containers behind me.

As I ran I saw Bell's thigh explode in a geyser of blood and flesh and he went down on one knee. Jackson grabbed one of the pistols the two policemen had dropped and headed towards the open door of the container and Nancy darted through the door that led into the offices.

As I vanished into the alley I snapped off one quick shot in the direction of Lambretta's men, and was heartened to hear a scream as the lucky shot went home.

I hoped that my good luck held.

Bullets and shotgun pellets were spanging off the metal behind me as I skidded to a halt in the shadows beyond the reach of the ceiling lights and out of the line of fire. I checked my arm. The bullet had gone straight through the muscle at the top and out the other side. It was bleeding, but not too badly, but I still needed to clot the blood. Quickly I put down my gun, shucked off my jacket, ripped the tail of my shirt off and bound the length of material round my bicep, knotting it with my right hand and my teeth. It wasn't perfect and it was starting to hurt by then, but it would have to do.

By the time I'd tugged on my battered leather jacket again, now accessorized by two holes in the sleeve, one a neat roundel, the other ragged and bloodstained, the firing had all but stopped. I looked down the alley in the direction I was heading. It was a dead end. I couldn't go forward and I couldn't go back. I looked round desperately, then my eyes roved towards the roof and I saw that the ladder that ran up the side of each container almost touched the one above, forming one long ladder to the top of the stack, and I decided that the only way was up.

I stuck the Browning into the waistband of my blue jeans, and using mostly my right arm, and favouring my left which was beginning to give me serious gyp, I started to climb the ladders. It was a bastard trying to drag myself up one-handed and when I reached the top I lay gasping for breath on the dusty roof of the top container.

After a moment I scuttled across and peered down at the floor of the warehouse.

The guard was lying rolled up into a ball where he'd fallen, Lambretta's men were spread out behind cover, except for one who lay still just outside the door. My shot had been a good one, but probably wouldn't put me into Lambretta's top ten. Not that I was going to lose a lot of sleep over that. Bell was lying on this side of the money container with his back against it and even from a distance it was obvious that he was losing a lot of blood from his leg wound. There was no sign of Jackson and Nancy, until Jackson stuck one hand out from behind the door of the container itself and fired.

Lambretta's men returned fire and Jackson's hand vanished.

Then the door to the inner foyer of the offices opened and the guard who'd let us into the building, another uniformed man I hadn't seen before, the guy in the blue shirt who'd operated the crane, and Nancy were shoved through. Nancy had lost her gun and from the look of her face had got a good clout for her pains.

Behind the four came Lambretta and John Duncan, his minder from Romford who belonged to the gun I was holding and who I'd kicked in the bollocks back at Lambretta's gaff. They were both both carrying automatics.

Shit, I thought. Why can't anything I do ever go right?

67

'Stop firing,' Tony Lambretta ordered, and a hush fell over the warehouse as his men obeyed, and I wondered where the hell Crazy Larry and his troops were, and how long we had before the law arrived to find out who was shooting the shit out of the outer suburbs.

'Sharman!' screamed Lambretta. 'Where the hell are you? Come out where I can see you, or I shoot the bitch in the back of the head.'

Much as I disliked Nancy I couldn't let that happen. Not right then. She had some information I needed to know, and she had to be alive to tell me.

I drew a bead on Lambretta's chest with the Browning and almost squeezed the trigger. But knowing how good a shot I am, there was more chance I'd blow the head off one of the hostages if I fired, so I put up the gun and shouted, 'Up here.'

All heads moved in my direction.

'Come down,' ordered Lambretta. 'And you, in the box. Throw out your gun and come out.'

'You can shoot her for all I care,' shouted Jackson.

'It ain't her I'm going to shoot if you don't come out,' said Lambretta. 'It's your pal, the other copper, and then you.'

There was a pause and then Jackson's gun came through the door and clattered to the floor and he came out with his hands up.

Lambretta's men got to their feet, and one of them

238

tugged Philip Bell up off the floor and supported him as he dragged his injured leg across the floor to where Lambretta and Duncan were standing with their prisoners.

'Now you, Sharman,' said Lambretta. 'Throw your gun well clear. I don't want it going off by accident.'

Of course I could always have unloaded it, but an unloaded gun is no good to anyone, so I threw it right across the warehouse where it bounced across a pile of cardboard boxes, hit the wall, spun off and skidded across the floor.

'Now come down,' ordered Lambretta.

I did as I was told, favouring my left arm again on the ladders during my descent, and was met by one of Lambretta's boys when I reached the ground, who grabbed my injured arm so hard I almost passed out and then pushed me back to centre stage.

'So,' said Lambretta when we were all together, bloody but unbowed. At least I was. I couldn't speak for Nancy, Bell and Jackson. But then I had one final desperate ace up my sleeve, even if one of my sleeves had two bullet holes in it. 'Here we are at last. Johnny – check that container.'

Duncan gave me an extremely dirty look and went and did as he was told. He went into the container and came out a second or two later with a canvas bag in each hand. 'Looks like it, boss,' he said to Lambretta.

'Good,' said Lambretta with a thin smile. 'Terry, bring in the truck.'

One of his men nodded, put his gun away, and headed towards the artic and low-loader.

'So what's the deal?' I said to Lambretta.

'No deal. We take the cash and get out of here before the police arrive.'

'Nice plan,' I said. 'But I thought we were going to do a split.'

'We were. But I changed my mind. And you've killed one of my blokes.'

'Lucky shot,' I said.

'Not for him.'

'They were shooting at us.'

'Pity they aren't better shots. Why'd you start shooting, anyway?'

'It was her,' I said, nodding my head in the direction of Nancy. 'She got greedy and pulled a gun. When your blokes showed up she got the shakes and popped one off.'

'Bad mistake,' snarled Lambretta.

'So what happens to us?' I asked. 'You can't just kill us all.'

'Can't I?' said Lambretta.

'There's two serving coppers here. Don't you think someone might get a bit inquisitive if we *all* vanish and then turn up in little bits all over London.'

'That won't happen again,' said Lambretta. 'If you lot disappear, you disappear for good.'

'Says you,' I said. 'You didn't do a very good job with Harry Stonehouse.'

'You can't—' interjected Nancy suddenly. 'You can't do this.'

'No?' said Lambretta as the truck reversed through one of the main doors. 'Try me.'

'You can't. You promised.'

'Boss,' said Duncan. 'We'd better get a move on.'

'Well, get the sodding thing loaded, then.' He turned to the bloke from Firmin's in the light blue shirt. 'You get up in the control room and get that container on our loader.' He turned to another of his men, a big geezer in a MA1 jacket. 'You go with him, Tommy. Make sure he does it right first time.' The big guy nodded and pushed the geezer in the blue shirt towards the ladder that led to the control room.

'You promised her what?' I said to Lambretta, picking up on what Nancy had said to him.

'He promised me a share.' Nancy's face was white and she was trembling.

'When you sold Harry out to him, you mean,' I said. 'Don't think I didn't know.'

'No,' said Nancy.

'Yes,' I said. 'You must take me for a bigger mug than I thought, if you didn't think I'd worked that one out for myself. Did you think he'd blown you out? Is that why you got me involved?'

'I didn't know what he'd done. But I knew the money still had to be somewhere. How *did* you know it was me sold Harry?' she asked.

'When I went to Lambretta's place he called you "that bitch". So I knew he must know you.'

'Harry wouldn't tell me where the money was,' she said pleadingly. 'I didn't mean for him to be killed.'

'Bollocks, Nancy,' I said. 'You didn't give a damn. I bet the only reason you stayed with him was because of this money.'

'He promised me,' she wailed.

'Everyone promises, Nancy,' I said. 'And everyone breaks their promise. But I promise you this, duck. Harry was my mate even though I fucked him over myself. And you were right. I do owe him, and I'll make sure you go down for what you did to him.'

'No chance,' said Lambretta. 'Where you're going to no one will ever hear from you again.'

'I wouldn't count on it,' I said. Because above the rumble of the truck's diesel I heard another sound. The sound of motor-cycle engines coming down the Purley Way at high speed.

68

Lambretta heard it too and frowned. 'Company,' I said. 'Better get the kettle on.'

Everyone in the warehouse looked at one another in puzzlement as the sound of the engines got louder outside and headlights crisscrossed the service road that ran up towards the front of the warehouse.

'What the fuck?' said Duncan, nervously raising his gun as the bikers skidded to a halt outside, Crazy Larry in the lead on a chopped '47 Knucklehead Harley-Davidson. He sat at the head of the phalanx of Street Shit revving up his engine through the chrome dragpipes that adorned the back of the machine, and I saw that instead of a false hand on the end of his left arm, he now sported a silver hook that was clamped tight on to the clutch of the bike. With his right hand he drew a revolver from inside his jacket and cocked the hammer with his thumb.

'It's those bikers,' said Lambretta. 'Where the fuck did they come from? It's OK, I'll deal with them. Don't shoot.'

That wasn't part of the plan. The last thing I wanted was for the bad guys to get all matey and for Crazy Larry and his pals to give the truck a motor-cycle escort back to east London.

I took my chance in the confusion that the gang's arrival and Lambretta's announcement provoked. One of his men had picked up all the abandoned guns and stuck them on top of a packing case, but he was paying more attention to what was going on outside than to keeping an eye on them, and with two strides I was next to him, picked up the Browning, cracked him round the back of the neck with the barrel and fired three shots into the pack of leather-clad riders who were blocking anyone's exit from the warehouse.

That was when all hell broke loose.

At least one of the wild shots hit a soft target and one biker toppled off his steed and lay writhing on the tarmac, as I grabbed one of the police Webleys, stuffed it into my pocket, ducked down behind the packing case for cover and started firing at any target I could see.

The bikers returned fire, their first volley chopping Bell to the ground and cutting another of Lambretta's men off at the knees. Nancy was left standing as all around her dived for cover. 'Nancy!' I screamed. 'Get over here.'

She looked at me in a panicked way, stepped back, then changed her mind and walked forward, straight into a round from someone's gun. It hit her on one side of her head, blowing a hole the size of a baking potato out of the other, and spraying hair, bone, blood and brains against the container closest to her. Her legs buckled and she fell face forward.

Tough shit, Nance, I thought. But the wages of sin are death, as I might very soon be finding out.

'Sharman!' I heard a voice shout from my right in a lull in the firing. 'Sharman. Over here.' It was Jackson. 'Give me my sodding gun,' he said.

'So's you can shoot me?'

'So's I can shoot some of those bastards. Not you. Jesus, where's the law?'

'You're here,' I said dryly.

'Not me. The locals. For Christ's sake, we've been

making enough fucking commotion over the last ten minutes.'

'It's quiet round here,' I replied. 'No fucker lives here any more. It's all supermarkets and computer warehouses.'

'There's someone in the pub over the way.'

'Probably pissed,' I said, and I reached up grabbed the other Webley and tossed it to him, and more bullets slammed into the case which I was hiding behind. Fuck it, if he was going to shoot me he was going to shoot me, but one extra gun could make all the difference. 'And you're going to have a hell of a lot of explaining to do when the old Bill do get here . . . If we're still alive to see them,' I added.

'We could cook up a story, you and me,' he hissed as he fired from his cover, and thank God not in my direction. 'There's still a big reward being offered by 4F. We could split it.'

'Like you were going to give me and Nancy a share of the money?'

'We were.'

'Bollocks.'

'All right, we weren't. But this time I'm being straight with you.'

'And I just take your word?'

'I'm finished without it. This all looks very bad, Sharman.'

'Very bad,' I agreed with him. 'In fact I'd say we were totally fucked.'

'I'm getting out of here,' he said suddenly. 'Fuck this for a game of soldiers.'

'No. You'll never make it.'

'Give me cover,' he yelled, bounced up and started to zigzag towards the door to the offices.

It was only a matter of yards, but he was cut down by

half a dozen bullets and shotgun loads before he'd a quarter made it.

Me, I dived in the opposite direction and rolled under the low-loader attached to the back of the big tractor truck.

So now it was just me.

Just me, and my Browning which had five rounds left, and Bell's Webley fully loaded with six bullets.

Just me against at least a dozen men, probably more, presumably with plenty of spare ammunition, but not a lot of time. Surely to God someone had called the police by now. Then I thought of my portable phone, pulled it out of my jacket and dialled three nines. 'Emergency, which service do you require?' said a voice

'Police, quick,' and I gave the address, then cut off the operator before she could start asking questions.

I looked up through the thick girders that made up the floor of the low-loader to where the container was swinging gently above it as the guy in the control booth tried to drop it neatly into place.

Somehow I had to get out of there, but right in front of me was just a stack of more containers and a bare wall. But if the money container was loaded and the truck drove off then I'd be left in the middle of the concrete like a cockroach on a clean hanky. And about as easy to swat, so I had to make a move.

I rolled forward and popped my head out from under the trailer and tried to get the bottle together to make a run for it, when Lambretta appeared behind me, gun in hand, and climbed on to the low-loader. 'Stop right there,' he ordered.

Shit, I thought. This is it.

Then everything happened at once. Two of the bikers appeared around the front of the truck. One fired at

Lambretta and one fired at me, both missing by a mile. Tommy, Lambretta's man who'd climbed up into the control room with the geezer in the blue shirt, swung out of the doorway up there and fired at the bikers, knocking one off his feet. The other fired up at him just as Lambretta put a bullet in his back so that the shot starred the control room window and the geezer in the blue shirt ducked down. The container that was still swinging maybe five feet above the low-loader dropped like a brick, and Lambretta made one desperate cry before he was squashed flat as a bug by the weight, and I saw blood begin to drip down from where he'd been kneeling and pool on the concrete floor.

I felt like throwing up, but then Tommy started shooting in my direction so I dived back around the corner of the container, which was when Crazy Larry spotted me.

Terrific.

'You!' he screamed.

'Hi, Larry,' I shouted back. 'Need a hand?'

He fired off two shots at me and I ducked back again and fired at Tommy who threw himself into the control room as Larry revved up his bike and with a scream of tyres skidded round so as to get a clear shot at me.

Fuck. Would this never end?

Crazy Larry skidded his bike to a halt in front of me. There was a red glint in his eye that perfectly matched the cellulose that coated his petrol tank. He revved up the bike with his good hand and with the metal claw worked the clutch, and the front wheel of the bike lifted as he did a wheelie straight at me, the single eye of his headlight transfixing me in its beam.

I bent my legs into a crouch, brought up the Browning in my right hand and fired straight at the centre of the light. The glass exploded and the bullet smashed through to the petrol tank, igniting it in an explosion of metal and red hot fuel, and Larry was blown upwards into the roof of the warehouse where the metal claw of his left hand caught in one of the pulleys of the lift mechanism and he swung there burning brightly like a steak on a barbecue as his bike veered off past me and hit the articulated tractor amidships just by the fuel tank. Immediately the sprinkler system in the ceiling came on, dousing everyone in water. But it was too late for the truck. The remaining petrol from Larry's bike flared across the bodywork and ignited the diesel in its tank and with a huge explosion the truck blew, throwing me face forward across the concrete floor.

69

I ended up in a tangle of arms and legs and hot air that stank of burning diesel, and the water that cascaded down from the ceiling next to the injured body of John Duncan, who was still clutching the two canvas bags he'd rescued from the money container. Pain seemed to encompass my whole being. Far away in the distance I finally heard the scream of sirens.

I dragged myself to my feet and looked down at Duncan as he looked back up at me. 'It's all over, John,' I said. 'The chicken's come home to roost. Harry can rest easy now.'

I didn't feel anything for Duncan then, or any of the others. Nothing. Not hate or love or disgust or pity. Not a sodding thing.

But he wouldn't leave it alone. He had to keep on, and from somewhere he produced a gun and tried to point it at me but his hand was wobbling so much that I just laughed and kicked it out of his grip.

'You just don't know when to quit, do you?' I said.

But then nor did I.

And I was damned if I was going to stick around for the post mortem.

He stared at me as I grabbed the sacks, zipped up my leather jacket and stuck them down the front, then looked round at the carnage that was all that was left of the warehouse, wiped the wet hair off my forehead and headed for the door to the offices.

It was the only way out that I could see, as the truck was burning fiercely and blocking my way to the front of the building.

I hit the door hard, spun left through the other entrance into the darkened reception and shot shit out of the glass door out into the parking lot with the last bullets from the Browning. It was strengthened glass and only webbed, so I had to kick the stuff out of the frame before I could escape. Outside, the sound of sirens was louder and I felt that I'd just about had it, when from around the corner came the growl of a big bike engine and seconds later I saw one of Larry's cohorts come slowly round with his lights off as if looking for a place to hide.

A bike. A sodding bike. Just what I needed, because the keys to Nancy's car were back inside, hidden in her bag which was God alone knew where. Maybe burnt to a frazzle in the fire, maybe just lying somewhere out of sight. And that left me without transport, and the sound of the sirens was getting louder by the second.

I pulled the Webley from my pocket and as the bike got closer I stood away from the wall and said, 'Gimme the bike or I'll shoot your fuckin' head off.'

I saw the guy clearly in the splash of light from the front of the building. I saw him think about revving up and going for it, and I said, 'Not in your dreams, pal, I'll knock you straight off the sodding thing and take it anyway.'

'Listen, man . . .'

'Gimme the bike,' I repeated, and with a look of disgust he dismounted. 'You armed?' I asked. 'Come on, gimme.'

He pulled some huge automatic out of his pocket and I took it and slid it into mine. 'Now fuck off,' I said. And he did.

I jumped on the bike and tried to remember how to ride

it. Christ, it had been years since I'd ridden one, and that was nothing like as powerful as this one, a big trial bike. A Kawasaki KLX with a six-fifty cubic capacity lump.

Still, here goes, I thought, and I put in the clutch, revved up hard, toed the gear lever into first, dropped the clutch in and took off. I drove round the corner and saw why the biker hadn't made good his escape. There were a bunch of police vehicles drawn up in front of the warehouse, and at the end of the service road, effectively blocking the exit was a Rover 600 police car. The building to my left was burning fiercely and I could hear more sirens in the distance. Probably the fire service, I thought, but I couldn't wait for the coppers to move. I had to get out, and get out now. To the left of the car was the empty gatehouse, then the fence topped with lethal razor wire, and to the right just more fencing. There was only one way out. A suicide rap, but I had no choice.

I idled the engine for a second, then went back into first and powered the bike across the tarmac, changing up to second, then third and bringing the bike's speed up to about fifty. I could see the the faces of the coppers behind the windscreen of the Rover as the bike's speed increased and I leant forward over the wide handlebars of the Kwacker and twisted the throttle to give myself even more revs.

I took one split second to slap on the headlight to full beam before leaning even further forward as I yanked the front wheel up with all my strength and did a wheelie for the last few yards before the front wheel of the bike hit the car's bumper, then its bonnet, then its windscreen and I thanked God for the teardrop design of modern cars, before the bike lifted clear and I was heading straight upwards towards the night sky. I saw the gatehouse below me and a strand of razor wire tore at my jeans, then I was above the fence, standing high on the Kawasaki's pegs, and I gave a shout of pure exultation at being there so close to the stars, before the bike started to slip away and I fought it straight, throttled back, and the rear wheel hit the pavement with a bang so loud I thought I'd burst the tyre or wrecked the mono shock, and the seat came up and almost turned my bollocks to mush, and I threw my weight backwards. The front wheel went down hard and the bike wobbled along the pavement and over the kerb and I changed up to fourth and sped along the Purley Way in the direction of central London humming the theme from *The Great Escape* as I went.

Steve McQueen, eat your heart out.

70

Jack Robber didn't have to see what happened on TV. Not that night at least, although the big fire at the security firm was reported extensively the next day and the following few. Firmin's customers freaked in front of the gutted building in technicolour. I know because I watched. God alone knows what some of them had hidden away there. Serves them right, the crooked bastards.

No. I told him myself. And I didn't disappear like he'd feared. Not for good, to be found in black plastic sacks at some later date. Although I did disappear for a bit until things cooled down. But at least he knew I was doing OK, and holding folding.

I rode to Dalston on the bike I'd stolen, the two bags of cash keeping me warm under my jacket, and the slipstream from the ride dried me, although I knew I looked like a scarecrow.

I stopped on the way at the twenty-four-hour coffee stall beside Waterloo Station where they'll serve anyone, no matter what they looked like, and I gobbled down a sausage sandwich and a plastic cup of tea, and they both tasted delicious. While I was there I keyed Diane's phone number into my portable. She took a long time to answer. 'Hello,' she said eventually.

'Hi. It's me.'

'Nick. Are you all right? I was worried.'

'Worry not,' I replied. 'Everything's worked out.'

'You've finished the job.'

'More or less. But whether it's more of a mess now than when I started is debatable.'

'And you're out of trouble.'

'I will be. Listen, Diane. I've got some money. How much I'm not sure. But I think it's a fair amount. Enough to get us away and keep us away for a bit.'

'Away where?'

'Wherever you want. I've got my passport. We could be in the Bahamas in a day or so. The States. Europe. Africa. Asia. Anywhere.'

'I don't think so, Nick.'

I couldn't believe what I was hearing. 'What do you mean?' I said.

'I've been thinking. It's been fun, it really has. But I don't know if I want to live like you.'

'What's wrong with the way I live?' Christ, by the state of me, that should've been obvious. It was to anyone but a fool, but I've never claimed to be that bright.

'Have you got a couple of hours?' she asked.

'I see,' I said. Although I really didn't, and later I decided that was more my problem than hers. 'So you don't want to come?'

'I do and I don't. But on consideration I think I'm more cut out for the quiet life.'

I sighed. Shit happens. But why does it always have to happen to me?

'I could come round. We could talk,' I said.

'I don't think so, Nick. You take the money and run. That's your style. But I don't want to be on the run with you.'

'I have to go away, Diane. You know that, don't you?'

'I know. And I know I'm going to regret not going with you.'

I made one last appeal. 'Think of all that photocopying you'll avoid at the office.'

'I think about it all the time. But on consideration...' She didn't finish the sentence.

'Diane,' I said. 'I understand. At least I think I do. You've been great...'

'Don't, Nick. You'll make me cry.' But I think she already was, and I know I was damn close myself.

'OK, honey,' I said. But by then she'd hung up, and I didn't call back. What would've been the point?

When I arrived at the hospital I was dirty and smoke-stained and covered in blood from my wound. The perfect disguise.

I dumped the bike out front, took the moneybags and climbed the stairs to the third floor where the red-headed sister was on duty. 'Is Jack Robber awake?' I asked.

'What have you been doing to yourself?' she asked back.

'Police business,' I said.

'You're not police.'

'Aren't I?'

'No. And the photograph on that warrant card looked nothing like you.'

'But you let me in.'

'I talk to your friend a lot. He told me to expect you the first day he was down here. He said you'd get in somehow.'

I shook my head. Life was full of surprises.

'You are Nick, aren't you?' she said.

'That's right.'

'Nice to meet you again,' she said. 'My name's Rosemary, by the way.'

'Pleased to meet you, Rosemary,' I said.

'He's awake,' she said. 'Go on in. He's watching television for some reason.'

And he was.

'It all worked out, Jack,' I said, throwing the bags on to his bed.

'Christ,' he said. 'You look a state.'

'I'll survive. Open the bags. If they're stuffed with newspaper, we're fucked.'

But they weren't. One of them contained thirty-two bundles of tattered notes in paper wraps marked '50×£20". The other, thirty-two bundles of the same. Sixty-two thousand quid. Not as much as we'd hoped, but not bad. 'Split it in half,' I said.

'I can't take it. I did nothing.'

'You did a lot. And we had a deal. I stick by my word.'

He looked at me and shrugged. 'If you insist,' he said, and put thirty-one bundles of cash back in each bag, and put one of them in the drawer of his locker. 'Are you OK?' he asked when he'd finished.

'Just about.'

'What are you going to do?'

'Take it on my toes. Get lost for a bit.' I held up the other bag. 'This should keep me going for a bit.'

'Look me up when you get back. If you come back.'

'I will,' I said.

'And maybe we can get into some life-threatening situations again.'

'I'll look forward to it.'

'Good luck, Nick.'

'Thanks,' I said, shook his hand and left.

On the way out the sister was going off duty. 'Looks like you could do with a visit to casualty,' she said.

'No casualty,' I said.

'Then maybe you'd better come home with me and let me look after you.'

'Maybe I'd better, Rosemary,' I replied.

And I did.